D1361971

THE
CIRCUIT RIDER'S
WIFE

THE
CIRCUIT RIDER'S
WIFE

CORRA HARRIS

 BRISTOL
BOOKS
WILMORE, KY 40390

THE CIRCUIT RIDER'S WIFE
by Corra Harris
Published by Bristol Books

Originally published as *A Circuit Rider's Wife* in July 1910.

First Bristol Books Edition, February 1988
Second Printing, April 1990

Library of Congress Card Number: 87-73216
ISBN: 0-917851-10-2

Printed in the United States of America

BRISTOL BOOKS
An Imprint of Bristol, Inc.
P.O. Box 150 • 308 East Main Street • Wilmore, KY 40390
Phone: 606/858-4661 • Fax: 606/858-4972

To the Memory of
William

.

Preface

The nineteenth century in American church life belonged to evangelical Protestantism. More specifically, it belonged to Methodists and Baptists. With just a handful of adherents in the early 1800s, these groups claimed the frontier, initiated the Great Evangelical Awakening and then dominated religion during the country's westward expansion. By the end of the century fully a half of the American populace was identified with some form of these two denominational families.

Along the way some unique features were added to American religious life: the campmeeting, the gospel song, the Sunday school, the youth league, the song leader, the Amen corner, the altar call, the revival meeting, the mourner's bench, the Ladies' Aid Society, the temperance society, the prayer band and the missionary society.

By the end of the century the church was becoming part of American culture. The rough edges of frontier evangelicalism were being smoothed by education and sophistication. Methodists and Baptists moving up the social scale wanted brick churches with stained glass windows, massive pulpit furniture, robed choirs and printed programs in their worship services.

Except, that is, in the small towns and rural areas of such places as Mississippi, Indiana and West Virginia, where church life continued much as it had since the days of the early settlers.

Farmers and shopkeepers in these areas were quite happy with the religion passed down by their grandfathers and grandmothers. It was institutionalized frontier Christianity, and it carried well into the twentieth century. This is the brand of faith described by Corra Harris in *The Circuit Rider's Wife*.

I personally happened unto the book quite by accident—in a box of books at the auction of the belongings of an old preacher. I read a page, then another and finally the whole book, alternately stirred and amused. And I realized that Corra Harris was not only an entertaining storyteller, she was describing people I knew, or at least had heard about. I believe my great-grandparents are in that story someplace, as well as many of my ancestors. Furthermore, the Redwine Circuit bore an uncanny resemblance to another Methodist circuit I served as a student pastor many years later.

The Circuit Rider's Wife is the reprint of a book that originally ran in serial form in the *Saturday Evening Post* in 1910. It is a reflection on the life of Corra Harris, the fictionalized Mary of the book, the wife of a Methodist preacher in the South in the late 1880s. More than that, it is a tribute to country preachers of a by-gone era and their faithfulness to a God who had called them into his service.

Riley B. Case

Contents

Chapter 1

I Am Chosen Instead of the Prayer-Meeting Virgin

If you will look back over the files of the "Southern Christian Advocate," published at the time in Macon, Georgia, you will find the following notice—by a singular coincidence on the page devoted to "obituaries": "Married—Mary Elizabeth Eden to William Asbury Thompson. The bride is the daughter of Colonel and Mrs. Eden of Edenton; the groom is the son of the late Reverend Dr. and Mrs. Asbury Thompson and is serving his first year in the itinerancy[1] on the Redwine Circuit. We wish the young people happiness and success in their chosen field."

"Chosen field" had reference to the itinerancy, not matrimony. And that was my "obituary" if I had only known it. For after that, if I was not dead to the world, I only saw it through the keyhole of the Methodist *Discipline* or lifted and transfigured by William's sermons—a straight and narrow path that led from

---

1   Refers to the old Methodist practice of moving its pastors, "itinerating" them, every two or three years.

the church door to the grave.

But now, after an absence of thirty years, I am addressing this series of letters to the people of the world concerning life and conditions in another, removed from this one by the length of long country roads, by the thickness of church doors, and by the plate glass surface of the religious mind. They will record some experiences of two Methodist itinerants and whatever I think besides, for they are written more particularly to relieve my mind of a very great burden of opinions. For William has been promoted. He has received his Master of Divinity degree in the kingdom of heaven by this time, if there are any degrees or giving of degrees there, along with Moses and Elijah, and I doubt if there is a more respected saint in that great company. We buried him a year ago in the graveyard behind Redwine Church.

I was born in Edenton, a little white-and-blue town in middle Georgia, and my name was recorded in the third generation of Edens on the baptismal registry of St. John's Church there. William was born somewhere in a Methodist parsonage, and his name is probably written on the first page of the oldest predestination volume in heaven.

In Edenton the "best families" attended the Episcopal Church. It was a St. John's, of course, though why this denomination should be so partial to that apostle is a mystery, for his autobiography, as recorded in the New Testament, reads more like that of a camp meeting Methodist than any other disciple's. As a child the presence of the church there at the end of the shaded village street was real to me, like my mother's presence. I did not repent in it as one must do in a Methodist or Baptist church, but I grew up in it like a daughter in the house of the Lord. As a girl on Sabbath mornings I entered it with all the mincing worldliness of my young mind unabashed. Later I was "confirmed" in it and experienced some of the vanity of that high spiritual calm which attends quick conversions in other churches. And to this day there is something ineffably sweet and whimsically inconsistent to me in an Episcopal saint. The fastidious stamina of their spirituality which never interferes with their worldliness is so satisfyingly human. Piety renders them increasingly graceful in manners and appearance. In heaven I believe Episcopalian saints will be distinguished from all others by stiff ruffs worn around their redeemed necks.

But all was different in the church to which William belonged and in which he had been brought up for three generations. The "best families" are never in the majority there. You will find instead, besides a few "prominent members," the poor, the simple-minded, the ne'er-do-wells morally, who have always flocked to the Methodist fold for this pitying reason, because they find that, if fallen, it is easier to rise in grace according to the doctrines of that church.

So, while William's father and forefathers had been engaged in the tedious mercy of healing and rehealing these lame, indigent souls according to various hallelujah plans, my mother and foremothers had been engaged in embroidering altar cloths and making durable Dorcas aprons for the unknown poor. This made the difference in our natures that love bridged. That is the wonderful thing about love—it comes so tremendously new and directly from God to recreate in us, and it is so divinely unprejudiced by what our ancestors did religiously or sacrilegiously.

To all appearances it would have been better for William if he had chosen for his wife one of those pallid, prayer-meeting virgins who so naturally keep their lamps trimmed and burning before the pulpits of unmarried preachers. They are really the best women to be found in any church. They never go astray, they are the gentle maiden sisters of all souls, the faded feminine love-psalms of a benighted ministry who wither and grow old without ever suspecting that their hope was marriage, no less than it is the hope of the giddiest girl. However, a preacher rarely takes one of them for his first wife. It is only after he has been left a widower with a house full of children that he turns imploring love-looks in their direction. And whatever is true in other churches, it will be found upon investigation that most of the excellent stepmothers so numerous in the Methodist itinerancy have been selected from this class.

But William was not a widower; besides, love is the leveler of human judgments in such matters and the builder of new destinies. So I was chosen instead of the prayer-meeting virgin to be his wife—the happiest, wildest young heroine in the town.

We met by chance in the house of a mutual friend. I remember the day very well, so blue above, so green below, with all the roses in Edenton blooming. I was going to tea at the Mallary's. I wore a green muslin, very tight in the waist, but flaring in the skirt like the spring boughs of a young bay tree. I had corn-tassel hair and a complexion that gave my heart away.

Mrs. Mallary, a soft, matchmaking young matron, met me at the door and whispered that she had a surprise for me. The next moment we entered the parlor together. The room spun around, I heard her introducing someone, felt the red betrayal on my brow, and found myself gazing into the face of a strange young man and hoping that he would ask me to marry him. It was William, a college mate of Tom Mallary's, spending the night on his way to his circuit from a district meeting. He wore his long-tailed preacher clothes and looked like a young he-angel in mourning as he bowed and replied to me with his eyes that indeed he would ask me to be his wife as soon as it was proper to do so. This was sooner than any trustee or missions mother in his church would have suspected. For once a man is in love, his sense of propriety becomes naively obtuse and primitive.

There is little distinction between a preacher and any other man as a lover. William, I recall, courted me as ardently as the wildest young scamp in Edenton, and I was flattered and delighted to have melted the mortal man in a young minister, who always looked as if he had just risen from his knees. I do not know why women are this way about preachers, but they are, at least they were in my day, and later I discovered that the trait leads to curious complications. Meanwhile, I left the course of our true love all to William, feeling that a man who could smile like that must know what was proper. We were engaged in less than a week and married in a month. Only women are the conductors of protracted courtships.

Our wedding tour was a drive of twenty miles through the country to the parsonage on the Redwine Circuit. And the only one who had any clear impression of the day was the horse. I do not even recall the road except that it swept away like a white, wind-blown scarf over the green world, and that wild roses looked at me intimately from the fence corners as we passed. William had a happy amen expression, but neither of us was thinking of the living or dying souls in the Redwine Circuit. The horse, however, had gotten her training on the road between churches and did not know she was conducting a wedding tour. She was a sorrel, very thin and long-legged, with the disposition of a conscientious red-headed woman. She was concerned only to get us to the parsonage in time for the "surprise" that had been secretly prepared for our coming.

Toward evening the road narrowed and steepened and, looking up, we caught sight of it, a little wren of a house hidden between two green shoulders of the world. The roof sloped until one could touch the mossy shingles, and the chimneys on either side were like ugly, voluminous old women who rocked the cradle of a home between them and cheered it with the red heart of wood fires within.

In the valley below lived the people of Redwine Church. But the world was withdrawn and could only be seen at a great distance through the gateway of the two hills. One had the feeling that God's ancient peace had not been disturbed in this place, and this was a solemn, foreboding feeling for me as we reached the shadow of the big fruit tree in front of the house, and William lifted me lightly from the buggy, opened the door—it was before the day of burglars and locks in that community—and welcomed me home with a kiss that felt a trifle too much like a benediction.

There were two rooms; one was a bedroom, having a red, white and blue rag carpet on the floor and furnished with a homemade bed, a low rocking chair, a very straight larger chair and a mirror hanging over a table that was covered with fancifully notched blue paper. The other was the living room and contained a cedar water bucket and dipper on a shelf, a bread-kneading bowl, dishpan, pot and two skillets on another shelf near the fireplace, two split-bottom chairs, a table and a cat. The cat was a large, gray agnostic. He never acknowledged William's presence by so much as a purr or a claw, and I have noticed that the agnostic is the only creature living who can treat a preacher with so much contempt. We found him curled up on the window sill next to the milk pitcher, sunning himself.

William went out to put up his sorrel. I drew up a chair in front of the shelf containing the bread tray, dishpan, pot and skillets, sat down and stared at them with horror and amazement. Why had William not mentioned this matter of cooking? I had never cooked anything but cakes and icings in my whole life!

I was preparing to weep when a knock sounded upon the door and immediately a large, fair woman entered. She wore the most extraordinary bonnet on her huge head that was tied somewhere in the creases of her double chin with black ribbons. And, on a blue plate, she was carrying a stack of green-apple pies nearly a foot high. Catching sight of the half-distilled tears in my eyes as I arose to meet her, she set the pies down, clasped me in her arms and whispered with motherly tenderness, "I know how you feel, child; it's the way all brides feel when they first realize what they have done and all they've done to theirselves. But 'tain't so bad; you'll come down to it in less 'an a week; and you mustn't cry now, with all the folks comin' in. They won't understand."

She pointed through the open door and I turned in the shelter of her arms to see down the road a strand of people ascending the hill, dressed like fancy beads, each behind the other and each bearing something in her hands or on his shoulders—and William standing at the gate to welcome them.

"Who are they?" I asked in astonishment.

"It's a donation party," she said. "I come on ahead to warn you. Them's the members of the Redwine, Fellowship and Macedonia churches, bringin' things to celebrate your weddin'. I'm Glory White, wife of one of the trustees at Redwine, and we air powerful glad to have you. So you mustn't cry till the folk air all gone or they'll think you ain't satisfied, which won't do your husband any good."

That was my first lesson in suppressing my natural feelings. As the years went by I had more lessons in it than in anything else. And I reckon it is not such a bad thing to do, for if one's natural feelings are suppressed long enough one develops supernatural feelings and feels surer of having a soul.

The donation party poured in, Sister Glory White and I standing between the kitchen table and the fireplace to receive them. William acted as master of ceremonies, gravely conducting each man and woman forward for the introduction. Everyone called me "Sister Thompson" and laid a "donation" on the table in passing. I was not aware at the time of their importance, but as William only received two hundred and forty-five dollars for his salary that year we should have starved but for an occasional donation party. In fact, they are smiling providential instances in the memory of every early Methodist itinerant.

Upon this occasion they ranged from bed quilts to hams and sides of bacon, from jam and watermelon rind preserves to flour, meal and doilies. One old lady brought a package of Simmons' Liver Regulator, and Brother Billy Fleming contributed a long twist of "dog shank"—a home-cured tobacco. The older women spread the food for the "infare," as the wedding dinner was called, upon the table, and we stood about it to eat amid shouts and laughter and an exchange of wit as good-natured as it was horrifying to bridal ears.

"So," said a huge old Whitman humorist whom I afterward identified as Brother Sam White, as he clasped both my hands in his, "this is Brother Thompson's new wife"—as if I were one of a series—"you are welcome, ma'am. He's been mightily in need of a wife to perk him up. He's a good preacher, but sorter like my young horse Selim. There ain't a better colt in the country only he don't show it; spirit's too quiet unless I lay a cuckle burr under his tail. And your husband, ma'am, what he says is good, but he don't r'ar and pitch enough. He can't skeer young sinners around here with jest the truth. He must learn to jump up and down and *whallop 'em* with it!"

All this was delivered in a bellowing voice that fairly shook the feathers in my hat. And it indicates the quality of William's ministry and the ideals of his congregation.

Chapter 2

I Build For Myself a Monument More Enduring Than Brass

As Sister Glory White had predicted, I "came down to it" at once and soon learned to perform the usual feminine miracles in baking and cooking. Our happiness did not differ from the happiness of other young married people except that it was abashed morning and evening with family prayers—occasions when Thomas, the cat, invariably arose with an air of outraged good breeding and withdrew to the backyard.

William had long, active, itinerating legs in those days, a slim, graceful body, a countenance like that of Sir Walter Raleigh and eyes that must have been like Saint John's. They were blue and had in them the "far, eternal look." And in the years to come I was to learn how much the character of the man resembled both that of the cavalier and the saint. Also, I was to learn that it was no light matter for one's husband to have descended from an ecclesiastical family that had found its way up through church history by prayer and fasting.

A Presbyterian may make the most abiding forefather because his doctrinal convictions are so strong they prenatally crimp the morals of those who come after him; and it may be that a Methodist ancestor counts for less in the third and fourth generation because his theology is too genially elastic to take a Calvinistic grip upon posterity, but it is certain that he will impart a wrestling-Jacob disposition to his descendants which nothing can change. So it was with William; he was often without "the witness of the Spirit,"[1] but I never knew him to let his angel go (cf. Gen. 32:26). He had a genius for wrestling in prayer as another man might have for writing great poetry. His words flew together like a flock of birds when he fell upon his knees, and rose like mourning doves to heaven, or they would be like high notes out of a black- Saul mood of the soul, and then they thundered forth from his lips as if he were about to storm the gates of paradise. And sometimes, in the dramatic intensity of his emotions, he would ask for the most terrifying things.

As we knelt together there in the quiet little house with no one near for help but the hills, I was, at first, alarmed lest heaven should take him at his word, for if half his petitions had been granted we could not have lived in this world. We should have been scattered like the fine dust of a too-great destiny. But presently, when nothing fearful happened during the night, I learned to have more confidence in the wisdom of God and less in William's. With him prayer was simply a spiritual obsession based upon a profound sense of mortal weakness and very mystifying to his young wife, who had cheerfully said her prayers from a book night and morning with an easy conscience.

The Saturday after our marriage I accompanied him to the Redwine Methodist Church, his regular appointment. It was the custom then to have preaching Saturday and Sunday. The church was set back from the road in a dim forest of pines, black

1   Means a sense of inward spiritual confirmation.

and mournful. Here and there horses and mules bearing saddles or dangling harnesses stood slipshod in the shade, switching their tails at innumerable flies. Near the door was the group of men one always sees about a country church on meeting days. They are farmers who have an instinct for the out-of-doors and who, for this reason, will not go in till the last moment.

Beyond the church in thicker shadows lay its dead beneath a colony of staggering gray stones. Upon one grave I remember, where the clay was freshly turned, there was a bouquet of flowers—love's protest against the sonorous sentence, "earth to earth and dust to dust," which the other graves confirmed. The pine needles lay thick above them, and not a flower distinguished them from the common sod. They had the look of deeper peace, the long, untroubled peace of sleepers who have passed out of the memory of living, worrying men. These chuchyards for the dead were characteristic features in country circuits, and I mention this one because ever after it seemed to me to be just inside the gateway of the Methodist itinerancy, and because, in the end, it came to be the home-place of my heart.

I had never before been in a Methodist church. A certain Episcopalian conceit prevented my straying into the one at Edenton. And I was shocked now at the Old Testament severity of this one. There was no compromise with human desires in it, not a touch of color except the brown that time gives unpainted wood, not an effort anywhere to appeal to the imagination or suggest holy imagery. Only the semi-circular altar rail about the narrow box pulpit suggested human frailty, prayer and repentance. On the men's side—the law of sex was observed to the point of segregation in all our churches—there was a sprinkling of men with strong, red, craggy faces who appeared to have the Adamic nature highly developed in them that seemed to set them back in the garden of Eden and hide them from God because of their sins. On the other side there was more lightness, more life and hope expressed in the faces of the younger women. But in the faces of the old there was the same outdone look of fallen humanity facing God.

There was no service, from the standpoint of my Episcopal rearing; just a hymn, a prayer and then William read his text, the Beatitudes—all of them. I have since heard better sermons on one of them, but the figure of him standing there behind the high pulpit in the darkened church with his eyes lifted, as if he saw angels above our heads, has never faded from my memory, nor have the faces of the old women in their black sunbonnets upturned to him, nor the drooping shoulders of the old men sitting with bowed heads in the Amen Corner. Somehow there was a reality about the whole scene that we did not have at home with all the fine music and heaven-hinting accessories.

William had reached the promise to the blessed peacemakers in the course of his sermon, the vision-seeing calm growing deeper in his eyes, when suddenly a woman on the front seat stood up, laid her sleeping infant on the floor with careful deliberation, took off her black calico bonnet, stepped into the aisle, slapped her hands together and began to spin around and around upon her toes with incredible speed. Her homespun skirt ballooned about her, the ruffle of her collar stood out like a little frill of white neck feathers. She had a fixed, foolish expression, maintained an energy of motion that was persistent and amazing, and gave out at regular intervals a short, staccato squeal that was scarcely human in sound.

Not a word was spoken; William himself was silenced as he watched the strange phenomenon. And I have often wondered since at the quality of that courage in an otherwise shrinking country woman which could cause her to rise, taking the service out of the preacher's hands as serenely as if she had been sent from God. And this is what she really believed. And every other member of the congregation, including William, shared the belief that she had an extraordinary blessing that day.

After all, it is a tremendous blessing to believe that one's God is within immediate blessing distance. In this connection I venture to add that it has always seemed to me a lack of comprehension which gives the Methodists the chief reputation for having an emotional religion, and it is certainly cheating the Episcopalians. For every time the service is read in an Episcopal church the congregation shouts the responses, quietly, of course, and by the book, but it is shouting just the same, and with a beseeching use of words both joyful and agonizing that surpasses any sporadic shouting of the Methodists.

After the sermon we had dinner on the grounds, for this was an all-day meeting with another service at the end of the day. And Saturday dinner on the grounds of a Methodist church thirty years ago was a function that appealed to the threefold nature of man as nothing else I have ever seen. Socially speaking, all the best people in the community were present; the real best people, you understand. Spiritually, it was an occasion hallowed by grave conversation; for were we not within the shadow of God's house, in the sacred presence of the dead? It was gruesome if you had an Episcopalian temperament, but certainly it was conducive to good breeding and sobriety. But more particularly, there was the dinner itself set out of huge hampers on white cloths that appealed to the natural primitive man simply and honestly, without a single pretense of delicacy to hide the real sensuality of the human appetite.

On this day an abundance of food strewed the ground, from Sister Glory White's basket to Sister Amy Jurdon's and Sister Salter's. There were biscuits the size of saucers and of the thickness of bread loaves, hams, baked hens, roasted pigs, more biscuits, cucumber pickles six inches in length, green-grape pies, custards of every kind and disposition, and cakes that proclaimed the skill of every woman in the church.

William advised me to eat as I had never eaten before or the women would think I did not like their cooking and would be correspondingly offended. I was expected to consume at least three of the great biscuits and everything else in proportion. Fortunately, I sat near a tangle of vines in which I discovered a dog was hiding, a hound who gazed imploringly at me through the leaves with the forlorn, backslidden-sinner expression peculiar to his species, as much as to say, "Don't tell I am here,

maybe then I'll get a few crumbs later on." I not only did not
tell, but I fed him eight of the biscuits, five slices of ham and
nearly everything else in reach of me except the cucumber pickles. I never saw a dog eat more furtively or so well.

Meanwhile, I was raising for myself a monument more en-
during than brass in the hearts of my husband's people as a
hardy woman who could make herself one of them. William,
who did not suspect the presence of the dog, grew faintly
alarmed, but I persevered till the last man staggered surfeited
from the feast. It was my first and, I may add, almost my only
triumph as a minister's wife on a backwoods circuit.

After the night service it was arranged that we should go
home with the Salters to spend the night. Sister Salter was one
of the Redwine saints, but Brother Salter was not a brother at
all—he was still in the world, a little, nondescript man with a
thin black beard and sad black eyes. But he was not proud of
his godless state, especially as it compared with his wife's
radiant experience; he was literally a humble sinner and showed
it. We took our places behind them in split-bottom chairs in the
one-horse wagon.

Sister Salter was still in her baptismal mood, and as we
rumbled on into the deepening twilight through the lovely
spring woods, she continued to sing snatches from the old
hymns. Higher and higher her fine treble voice arose till the
homing birds answered and every living thing in the forest felt
the throb of the poignant melody—everything except the baby
on her breast. It slept on as soundly as if it breathed her peace
into its soft little body.

Night had fallen when we reached the house, a one-room
log cabin.

"Light and go in," said Brother Salter. "I reckon the children
air all in bed. You 'uns kin ondress and git in while me and
Sally unhitches the horse."

We "lit" and entered the large room flooded with moonlight.
There was a bed in each corner, all occupied save one. This was
evidently the "company bed." We knew by its opulent feather

paunch, by the white-fringed counterpane and by the pillow-shams bearing dull mottoes worked in turkey-red thread. One could not tell the age of or how many persons were already a-sleep in the other beds; but judging from the number and varying sizes of the shoes that cluttered the floor beside them, there must have been a hearty dozen, ranging all the way from adolescence down to infancy.

It is needless to add that we were apparently asleep with the covers over my horrified head when the elder Salters entered. Where they slept is still a mystery. But we were awakened very early the next morning by the sound of Sister Salter's voice singing, "His loving kindness, oh, how good!" as she rattled the stove doors beneath the cookshed in the yard.

Three very young children were sitting half under our bed examining our shoes and other articles of apparel, and as many older heads stared at us from the opposite beds. My anguish can be better imagined than described, and the nonchalance with which William arose and pulled on his trousers did not add to my opinion of him. I afterward learned that nothing was more common than this populous way of entertaining guests, and that he had long since become hardened to the indelicacies of such situations.

Chapter 3

The Revival at Redwine

But this was only the beginning of social and spiritual surprises through which I passed. There was no culture among the people. They looked like the poor kin of the angels in heaven, and they really did live so far out of the world that no bishop had ever seen them. I was divided between horror and admiration at their soul-stretching propensities, and it is difficult to describe the shock with which I faced the perpetual exposure of their spiritual nakedness. It was a naive kind of religious indelicacy, like the unguarded ways of very young children.

Brother Jimmie Meadows would confess to the most private faults in an experience meeting, and if he did not, Sister Meadows would do it for him. They lacked the sense of humor which, being interpreted, is a part of the sense of proportion. They shrank from the illuminating quality of wit as if it were a sacrilege—this self-seriousness was even an important part of William's character. He put on solemnity like a robe when he was in the throes of thought.

The deadly monotony of Christian country life where there are no beggars to feed, no drunkards to reform, which are among the moral duties of Christians in cities, leads as naturally to breaking forth of what Methodists call "revivals" as did the back-slidings of the people in those days. So it came to pass that year at Redwine, when the "crops were laid by," that William faced his first revival, and I faced William. Spiritually speaking we parted company. He passed into a praying and fasting trance, and my heart was nearly broken with the loneliness. Praying and fasting did not agree with me, and William seemed to recede in some mystical sense hard to define, so that I became a sort of unwilling divorcee.

The revival was to begin at Redwine when suddenly the rumor reached us that Brother Tom Pratt, a prominent member, had back-slidden and that nothing could be done there in a spiritual way until he was reclaimed. He was a large, fair, thick-lipped man with a long straw beard hanging under his chin, and he was said to be mightily gifted in prayer. But his besetting sin was strong drink, and he had recently been drunk. The simplicity with which William went about reclaiming him as a part of the preparation for the coming revival seemed to me almost too premeditatedly spiritual.

The revival proceeded, at first with awful chilliness, at length with flickering warmth. At last, after a very moving sermon on the prodigal son, the altar suddenly filled with penitents. I have often thought of it, the tenderness with which the good God founded the Scriptures so they would fit the human heart to the uttermost generations of men. That story of the prodigal is the eternal love message from Him to us. Preach it anywhere and the aching, shamed, dissolute rebel in us trembles and wants to come home. Here in this hill settlement, where scarcely any man had been ten miles from where he was born, it seemed that a hundred had been secret vagabonds in the terrible "far country."

When the altar was full to suffocation William called on Brother Tom Pratt to "lead us in prayer." And he led us through a long night into the very morning of God. I wish it were the fashion to call more often on outbreaking sinners to pray in church. Usually they have a stronger sense of the presence of the Lord than the long-winded saints do; and many a time since that night have I listened to the heaven-turning eloquence of better men in prayer, but never have I heard a nobler petition for the forgiveness of sin.

The church was a darkened space rimmed with light from tallow candles standing on wooden brackets around the walls, and the space was filled with the bowed forms of men and women. Near the pulpit there was more light falling upon the dejected figures of the penitents clinging to the altar rail. Within the rail, kneeling facing them, William's face gleamed like the death mask of prayer.

There was a silence; then a voice arose from somewhere out of the deeper shadows, timid, beseeching at first, like a sad messenger of the outer darkness who had known all the torments of hell and trembled now before the throne of heaven. But as the bearer of the petition gained courage from his very woes, the volume of his voice increased until it filled the church. The rafters shook, and sinners fell prostrate in the aisles. This, however, was only the beginning. The great opera of Brother Pratt's spirit went on like a rude Wagnerian measure until none could resist it. Men arose from their knees shouting. Finally the prayer-maker, who had risen in his passion and stood praying with his hands above his head, reaching visibly for salvation, fell exhausted to the floor.

The scene is no less amazing to me now as I recall it than it was that night thirty years ago as I sat, a trembling bride, in the remotest corner praying privately and fervently that the Lord would spare me the sight of William taking part in it. I felt that if he did I should ever after have some earthly fear of him. If preachers could only preach without thrusting us up too close to the awful presence of God before our time!

It was the custom in those days always to conclude a Methodist revival with a "love feast"; you cannot have it where you have not had an old-fashioned revival. One of the coldest functions I ever attended was a so-called "love feast" in a fashionable Methodist church at the end of a series of meetings.

The men wore tuxedos and the women wore party gowns, high-necked of course, on account of it being a church affair. And the only difference between that and any other social function was that a good many people were present whom the fashionable members never invited to their own homes and whom they treated with offensive cordiality on this occasion.

But at the end of the revival at Redwine there was a true "love feast." A great crowd had assembled, due to the honorable curiosity in the neighborhood to know who would "testify," who would confess his fault or proclaim that he had forgiven some brother about a line fence between their farms. It was indeed a sort of Dun and Bradstreet opportunity to know the exact spiritual standing of every man and woman in the community.

William planned to hold the service in the evening out-of-doors under the great pines. Torches of pine wood furnished the illumination. William stood beside a small table facing the congregation, who were seated on the benches that had been brought out of the church. After a song and a prayer that must have made the old saints sit up on their dust in the graveyard behind the church to listen, William gave the customary invitation.

"Brethren and sisters," he said, "we have had a gracious meeting and a mighty outpouring of the Spirit. It is meet and proper for those who have been helped, who feel that their sins are forgiven, who aim to live a new life, to get up and say so, and thus burn the bridges behind them. Come out on the Lord's side so everybody can see where you stand! I leave the meeting open to you."

"Brother Thompson," said a gray old man with flour on his coat, "I feel that I have been blessed durin' this meetin', and I ask the prayers of all Christian people that I may continue faithful to the end!"

"Amen!" said William, and there were general grunts of approval, for the miller was known to be a wonderfully good man.

"Brother Thompson," said a strange, shaggy young Adam, "I feel that my sins are forgiven me and that I am a child of God. I ask the prayers of all Christian people that I may continue faithful." He was a moonshiner who had destroyed his whisky and cut up his own copper still and vats during the meeting. As he resumed his seat a little thin woman in a blue cotton dress sprang to her feet, hopped with the belligerent air of a fighting jaybird across the intervening space and lost herself in the arms of the regenerated moonshiner. She was his wife, the good woman who stayed at home and prayed for him of nights. Now she shouted and beat a tender tattoo with her little brown hands upon his bowed head.

"I jest can't help shoutin'," she cried. "I'm so glad he done it!"

He had "done it" three times before—reformed, only to fall again so soon as the corn was gathered in the fall. No one had confidence in him save this little blue-winged heart who loved him. It is no wonder women believe in God easier than anyone else does! They can believe with so little reason in men.

After this followed several triumphant testimonies. Sister Glory White began to shout sweetly and quietly in the Amen Corner, slapping her fat hands together and whispering softly, "Bless the Lord, O my soul! Bless the Lord, O my soul! And all that is within me, praise His holy name!"

Presently there was an interruption. William had made the mistake of confiding one of the torches to Brother Billy Fleming, a "holiness man." Suddenly he leaped into the air, shouting and brandishing his blaze in every direction.

The paroxysm of joy was short, however, and when quiet was restored in the deeper darkness—for Brother Fleming's torch had gone out—a tall man arose from near the middle of the congregation. He had a bushy brown beard, a little apostrophe nose, childish china-blue eyes and a thin high voice which gave the impression upon hearing it that he was at the very moment trying hard to squeeze through the eye of his needle, spiritually speaking. I recognized him as Brother John Henry, distinguished for having the most sensitive conscience of any man in the church. Now he stood with tears in his eyes, for a moment too deeply moved to speak. Everyone leaned forward, for it was always a matter of interest to know what else was troubling Brother Henry's soul. At last, in a quavering treble he confessed with the air of one doomed to suffer terrible disappointment.

"Brother Thompson, you know, all of you know, I try to be a good man. But the flesh is weak. I git tempted and fall into sin before I know it. I'm sufferin' remorse now because I set my old dominique hen twice and cheated her into hatchin' two broods of chickens without givin' her a day's rest between settin's! My remorse is worse because a man can't apologize to a hen or make restitution!"

Such rarefied confessions were common, and this was one of many occasions when I disgraced William by snickering in the solemn pause which followed.

However, these faded pictures of memory suggest but faintly any idea of the people with whom I began my life as a minister's wife. I can only show their narrowness. I am not able to give the shrill high notes of faith in their lives. They made an awful business of being good. And the contrast between them and the witty, mind-bred, spirit-lost people of the world was startling indeed, but more to their credit than some are accustomed to think.

Chapter 4

William As a Leader of Forlorn Hope

For spiritual beings, we do take with singular heartiness to the soil and spoils of this present world. The hope of immortality is more a fear than a hope with many of us. We do not like to see the open door of death that leads to it. So every good preacher is the shepherd of our misgivings, the leader of our forlornest hopes, the captain more particularly of men and women who are about to die or who are seeking heaven at last in a state of earthly disappointment and world exhaustion. I have rarely known a person in good health morally and physically, fortunately situated in life, who voluntarily sought the consolations of religion.

I reckon the Lord knew what He was about when He turned His back and let Satan fill creation with snares and pitfalls and sorrows and temptations. If we did not fall into so many of them we should never get the proper contrite spirit to seek of our own will and accord after salvation. He would have been obliged to thrust it upon us and we might have been no better than the angels, without the great privilege of sinning our own sins or choosing our own virtues.

William was especially qualified for this business of leading hope after it had done with all earthly ties. He was intellectually opposed to what we know as reality. He entertained in minutest detail convictions concerning the New Jerusalem, and he could give information about the Father's house as the old family homestead of the soul so definitely that one could see the angels on the gables and the Tree of Life shading the front yard. The simplest man in the congregation listened with enthusiasm and found himself recollecting it as if he were recalling scenes from a former life.

But eternity is a danger none of us can avoid, and it never seemed spiritually intelligent to me for Christians to struggle so in that direction. Indeed, they do not, really. That heaven-desiring enthusiasm is but the name of the pathetic courage with which they go to meet death because they have to go.

I recall the thanksgiving prayer of Brother Billy Fleming in this connection. In every experience meeting one part of his testimony was always in bold type—the ambition to be at home in glory and particularly to rest in Abraham's bosom. But when a long fever brought him almost within kissing distance of Abraham's beard he made a mighty prayer that God would spare his weak and unprofitable life. Not only that, but William was called in to add his own petitions, which he did throughout the night of the crisis of the fever.

I remained in the next room with Sister Fleming, a little silent saint who went about the world like a candle moving in a dark place merely letting her light so shine. When the night deepened and we sat in it, clasped hand in hand, listening to the prayer concert in the sick man's room, I ventured to propound a question.

"Sister Fleming," I whispered, "I can understand why you want Brother Fleming to live and why the rest of us do; but I can't understand why he has changed his mind so completely and wants so much to live himself. I have heard him say so often that he was not only ready and willing to go, but just longing to be with Abraham."

"Honey," she replied in the tone with which a mother speaks of the childishness of children, "them's one of the curiosities of the Christian religion, the things persons like Billy tell in experience meetings. I don't reckon the Lord takes the trouble to even forgive 'em, they air so foolish. I know Billy from A to Izzard, and, so far from layin' on Abraham's bosom, he couldn't git along with him till daybreak. He jest gits that talk out of his ambition and imagination, although humanly speakin' Billy is a tolerably good man, and I don't reckon the Lord will have any cause to fling off on him when his time comes. But you can jest set this down, nobody in his right mind feels the way most folks say they feel in an experience meeting!"

As a matter of fact, Brother Fleming made a public thanksgiving prayer at the altar in Redwine Church as soon as he was able to get out.

This deliverance from a woman of such beautiful integrity was a comfort to me. For while I endeavored to be a Christian along with William, I have never been religious. To feel consciously religious is, in my opinion, to be rather impertinent. This is my objection to the "holiness people"; they are presumptuous in professing a too-intimate likeness and relation to God. I have never seen a sanctified man or woman yet whose putty-faced spirituality bore nearly so noble a resemblance to Him as the sad, thunder-smitten soul of some sinner who had had his vision of unattainable holiness.

I am thankful that William was never guilty of the temptation to call himself "sanctified." Sanctification is a good thing to preach and a better thing to strive after, but the minute a man professes it he becomes less truthful and less intelligent spiritually, and he proceeds to develop along these lessening lines.

Still, while William did not outrage my reverence for him by a too-high profession, I found him hard enough to follow. When during the first year, Sabbath after Sabbath, I saw him quicken the spirit of his congregation with hymns and prayers and then, taking his text for a motto banner, start for the outskirts of eternity, I was probably the one person in his congregation who hung back for conscientious reasons. I looked at the weary people in the church with such sad hunger in their faces, and then I looked through the open windows at the fair fields spread like love promises of peace to us in this life, and it seemed to me that possibly they had missed the cue somewhere and I declined to make even a spiritual investigation of that country beyond where the scenes of William's sermons were always laid.

Very soon I also experienced a woman's fear that eventually I should lose some near and dear sense of my husband. There is, in fact, a highly-developed capacity for heavenly infidelity to earthly ties in most preachers and the martyrdom of forsaking father and mother and even his wife in the spirit appealed to his spiritual aspirations. Many a woman has been deserted in this subtle manner by her minister husband. But I kept the fear of it to myself, never encouraging this rarified form of piety in him by even opposing it. Meanwhile, I began to observe with genuine admiration his heroism in raising forlorn hopes.

This brings me to one of the most important duties of a circuit rider, that of piloting the dying through the last shallows of the great sea. There is where hope is the lowest and where William was bravest. Pastors of fashionable churches rarely perform this office now. It seems that an up-to-date church member regards dying as being so private as to suggest the idea that some disgrace is attached to it. The minister speaks cheerfully and conventionally of the hereafter as a rich and famous city with a beneficial climate. He congratulates the candidate for immediate residence upon his new citizenship and takes his departure without the risk of disturbing his temperature with a hymn of prayer. The proper time for both of these will be when he officiates later over the "remains."

I have sometimes wondered how a fashionable person feels who is obliged even to die by the doctor's orders and according to convention, repressing to the last those great emotions that have made us men instead of clods.

Far away in the country death brings more distinction. There, men and women have walked a lifetime in the fields, they have seen the sun rise and set, the stars shine, the rain fall, the corn grow—all by the will of God. And at the very last they are crowded by their great thoughts of Him, excited by the encroaching fact of His tremendous nearness. They need a priest, someone who has been "ordained" to lead them into the Presence. They have a sense of their ruggedness, their unkempt earthiness and their general unfitness for the great ceremony. The preacher must hold their hands until they cross the doorsill of heaven.

Now I will not say that William enjoyed officiating on these occasions, but they thrilled him, increasing his faith. And it touched me to the very heaven of my heart when I discovered that if the dying man was unconverted, an outright sinner, William was wont to omit the harder doctrines and generously lift him to the Lord in prayer upon the easy pledge of faith. The Methodists are especially prepared by the very softness of their creed to afford quick relief to the dying—just repent and believe in the Lord Jesus Christ and be saved.

Looking back through the years, across many, many graves, it seems to me I can see the footprints of William shining yet in the dark of death-nights as he journeyed forth to whisper hope into pale ears, and to offer his strange, heavenly consolation to those about to be left behind. Very soon after we were married there came a knock at the door one night and a voice crying, "Come quick, Brother Thompson, old Davy Dyer is dyin'. Doctor says he can't last till daybreak, and he's hollerin' for a preacher same as if he hadn't been against God all his life."

Davy Dyer was the blacksmith and the only infidel in the country, a grimy old iron worker with a white beard and an eagle's implacable eye. One of William's braveries was to go there to have his red-headed horse shod and to sit upon the edge of the anvil block while it was being done and gently try to wheedle him toward heaven. Now, at last, he was to have the best of the argument. Davy was dying, about to be turned out of the house and home of his spirit, and he wanted the preacher to help him find another. He must have another. No matter how intelligent a man is or how scientific his method, something in him can't reason his way back to the dust from which he was created.

The time was very short and William hurried away as if he had doves on his feet and the words of eternal life on his lips.

He returned in the opal dawn of the summer morning pale and weary but in his high ceremonial mood.

"He died in the faith," he answered calmly.

I had my doubts, my sniffing Episcopalian doubts, but the calm light upon his face, an incandescence that he managed from somewhere within, silenced me. I never meddled with the coals on William's altar. And not long after the penance of old Dyer I had an unexpected opportunity to observe how easy William made it for his people to "die in the faith."

We were living a perfectly ordinary day among the roses and sagebushes and bumblebees in our little garden when word came that Mrs. Salter had been suddenly stricken and was about to die "without the witness of the Spirit." There was a row of dahlias behind the blue-belled sagebushes requiring attention, and we had been so normally earth-happy digging about their roots. William had been so like other young men in his digressions that I could not help being depressed at the interruption. It seemed that some shadow of the other world was forever falling between us.

We came up out of our garden; William harnessed his horse, put on his longest-tailed black coat, changed his expression and we drove away on our sad mission. For custom required that the pastor's wife should accompany him upon such occasions. Her care was to look after the stricken surviving members of the family while he gave his attention more particularly to the passing one. She must be ready to do anything from cooking the next meal to shrouding the corpse.

The latter is a particularly garrulous business, and I was horrified to discover that it was so gruesomely entertaining to the women of the church and neighbors who helped. My first corpse was the young wife of a farmer who had died of "the fever," as usual. Sister Fleming and Sister Glory White had helped me "lay her out." And each vied with the other as to the number and condition of the bodies they had prepared for burial, incidentally comparing points between them and the present one. The grand dignity of the dead woman's face did not appall them, but it frightened me.

"O Sister White," I whispered, trembling and covering my eyes from the sight of them cackling about the dreadfully disheveled bed and its burden, "don't talk so before her. She looks so much above us!"

"Lor', child, you'll git used to it. They all have it, that grand look, when they air dead. It don't mean nothin'. Once I 'laid out' a bad woman; there wasn't another person in the settlement that would touch her, so I done it, and of all the corpses I ever put away she had the grandest look. It sorter staggered me till I thought at last it was maybe the rest that come to her after the pain of sinnin' had gone out of her body. But you'll not be so squeamish about the way folks look when they air dead after a while. We had one pastor's wife that helped lay out fourteen bodies. But that was the year of the epidemic," she concluded, leaning over to stretch the shroud sheet. Little did I think then that I was already upon the eve of an experience that would far eclipse the record of that other preacher's wife.

We found Sister Salter lying dim and white upon her bed, surrounded by her family and friends. And the supreme tragedy of the hour for them was not her approaching death, but it was that one who had testified so often and so victoriously of her faith had lost it at the crucial moment.

What followed is impossible to describe. It was not the terrible silence in the crowded room, not the battling breath and the shriveling features of the woman in the bed, not by contrast the green and happy calm of the world outside, but it was the awful voice of authority with which William spoke of things that no man knows that frightened and thrilled us. If he had called me like that from a grave where I had lain a thousand years I should have had to put on my dust, rise and answer him.

William sat beside the bed and looked as Peter must have looked at Dorcas as she lay dead in the upper chamber of her house at Joppa. It was not the text he quoted, nor the hymns he chanted, but it was the way he did it. Clearly he was adding his faith to her forlorn hope. We saw her face change as if she had risen and was treading the waters in her spirit to meet an invisible presence. The fading light of the summer day showed the same rapt look on it that was there when she shouted that first Sunday at Redwine, and she passed like a sudden gleam into the darkness of the coming night.

William's joy was beautiful to see, but I had a sense of intrusion as if I had parted the wings of some archangel and had seen more brightness than it was lawful for a mortal to behold. So long as we are on this earth it seems to me better to follow the example of Moses and turn our backs when the Lord passes by, so that we shall see only the glory of His hinder parts.

The death of Sister Salter marked the beginning of an epidemic, or rather the return of the same one they had had some years before. It swept through the community with such deadly results that not a family escaped. And I had another view of the ministerial character.

William spent all his time in the stricken homes of his people. It was not a sense of duty or conscience or courage that caused him to face the deadly disease with such fortitude, but it was the instinct of the shepherd for his flock. And he readily permitted me to accompany him with the curious indifference to consequences shown by those who have had their heads grandly turned by heavenly thoughts. Life meant little to him, immortality meant everything. He risked his own life and the life of his wife because it is the nature of the true priest to care more for his people than he does for himself or his wife, just as it is the nature of the good shepherd to lay down his life for his sheep.

At the end of three weeks we had buried half the membership of Redwine Church and had received the secrets of many passing souls. For a man cannot die with his secret in him. It belongs to history and will not be buried. One old woman, Sister Fanny Clark, who had been a faithful member of our church for years, confessed to William at the very last that she had always wanted to be a Baptist, but that her husband had been a Methodist and she had "gone with him."

"If I could have been put clean under the water when I j'ined and not had sech a little jest flung on my head, seems as if I'd feel safer now," she wailed. "And I've took the Lord's Supper with sinners and all kinds when it was in my conscience to be more particular and take it 'close communion' style like the Baptists. Besides, I have believed in the doctrine of election all my life, and I ain't noways sho' about mine now, although I've tried to do my duty." The fading eyes looked at us out of the old face sternly crimped with the wrinkles she had made working for God under an alien creed.

"My soul's never been satisfied, not for a single day, in your church with its easy ways and shiftless doctrines," she concluded faintly.

For once William was silenced. It was not an occasion upon which to vindicate Methodism in an argument. Neither did he have enough tautness of conviction concerning certain terrible doctrines to meet the emergency of her dogmatic needs. And so she passed without absolution to the mercies of a God who is doubtless sufficiently broad-minded to have such baptisms properly attended to somewhere in heaven.

Chapter 5

God's Annuals

But the dying are not the only ones who suffer most from sickness of their hopes. There are men with beautiful souls born with little devil seeds in them somewhere that grow like immoral perennials and poison the goodness in them. They are the people who backslide so often, who repent so thoroughly, and who flourish like green bay trees spiritually when they flourish at all. They are usually regarded as moral weaklings and it is the fashion of saints to despise them. This is because some righteous people now, as in Christ's day, are the meanest, narrowest-minded moral snobs the world can produce. Many of them are too mean even to afford the extravagance of a transgression. And rarely indeed do you see one with courage enough to erect himself again, morally, once he has fallen or been discovered as fallen.

But among the backsliders of the class I have mentioned you will find the bravest moral heroes of the spiritual world, men who have the courage to repent and try again with an enthusiasm that is sublime in the face of the lack of confidence expressed in them on all sides. They are a distinct class, and as we went on in the itinerancy I learned to call them God's annuals. And William never was more beautifully ordained or inspired than when he was engaged in transplanting one of those out of his sins again into the sweet soil of faith. He had a holy gardener's gift for it that was as naive as it was industrious.

I recall one of these annuals on the Redwine Circuit. He was a slim, wild young fellow with a kind of radiance about him; sometimes it was of the devil, but he always had it—an affable charm. He was blue-eyed and brown with a level look that hero warriors have. And that was his trouble. He was made for emergencies not for the long, daily siege of life. He was equally capable of killing an enemy or of dying for a friend, but he could not live for himself soberly and well for more than forty days at a time.

Still, he had a soul. I never doubted it, though I have often doubted if some of the ablest members in our church had them and if they were not wearing themselves out for a foolish anticipation if they expected eternal life.

It is possible for a man to behave himself all the days of his life without developing the spiritual sense. I do not say that such people do not have souls, but they are encased in granite and if they get to heaven at all the angels will have to crack them open with a jackhammer before they can find the thing these people kept for a soul.

But Jack Stark, our Redwine annual, was too much the other way. His soul was not enough inside of him. It was the wind in his boughs that blows where it listeth. Periodically he went on a "spree"; it was his effort to raise himself to the tenth power, because he had an instinct for raising himself one way and another. If at the end of a week he did not appear at the parsonage door, sober, dejected and in a proper mood for repentance, William went after him, plucked him up from somewhere out of the depths and proceeded at once to transplant him again in the right garden.

In all the years of his ministry I never knew William to lose hope in his annuals. He was always expecting them to become evergreens of glory. In dealing with them he had patience a little like the patience of God, never reproaching them or threatening them with the time limits of salvation in this world. No man ever had a sublimer skill in dealing with the barren fig-tree elements in human nature.

Years after this time John Stark became congressman from his district. And William died in the belief that he also became a "total abstainer." John probably was at the moment he told William so, but having studied the nature of spiritual annuals I may be pardoned my doubts. However, he will have nursery place in heaven, if for no other purpose than to furnish congenial employment to saints like William.

I have often wondered what would have happened if the prodigal son had been a daughter. Would the father have hurried out to meet her, put a ring on her finger and killed the fatted calf? I doubt it. I doubt if she would ever have come home at all, and if she had come the best he could have done would have been to say, "Go, and sin no more."

But "go," you understand. And all over the world you can see them, these frailer prodigals, hurrying away to the lost places.

In a rotting cabin in an old field five miles from Redwine lived one of them. Once a week she walked fourteen miles to the nearest large town to get plain sewing, and with this she supported herself and child. The field was her desert. For eight years no respectable woman had crossed it or spoken to her till the day William and I and the redheaded horse arrived at her door. She stood framed in it, a gaunt figure hardened and browned and roughened out of all resemblance to the softness of her sex. Her clothes were rags, and her eyes like hot, dammed fires in her withered face. William sprang out of the buggy, raised his hat and extended his hand.

"My wife and I have come to take dinner with you," he said.

"Not with me! Oh, not with sech as me!" she murmured vaguely. Then seeing me descend also, she ran forward to meet me, softly crying.

We stayed to dinner, a poor meal of corn hoecake, fried bacon and sorghum, spread upon a pine table without a cloth. But of all the food I ever tasted, that seemed to me the most nearly sanctified. It was with difficulty that we persuaded the lost Mary to sit down and partake of it with us. She was for standing behind our chairs and serving us.

After that she sat, a tragic figure, through every service at Redwine, even creeping forward humbly to the communion. She was not received, however, in any of the homes of the people. She might "go in peace"—whatever peace her loneliness afforded—that the Scriptures might be fulfilled and that was all. The "saints" would have none of her. This was not so bad as it seemed. She was free indeed. Having no reputation to win or lose she could set herself to the simple business of being good, and she did. The time came when the field changed into a garden and the cabin whitened and reddened beneath a mass of blooms.

But there was one man whom William could never lead when hope fell forlorn and the way seemed suddenly rough and dark. That was himself. This is why I cannot get over grieving about him wherever he is. Nothing that comes to him of light now can lighten those other days far down the years when he lost his way and had no one to preach to him nor lead him. For the one tragedy that marked the course of our lives in the itinerancy was not the poverty and hardships through which we passed, it was the periodic backsliding of William.

This is a pathetic secret that I never mentioned during his lifetime. I did not even know for many years that all Methodist preachers who are not hypocrites have these recurrent downsittings before the Lord. It grows out of nature's protest against the stretched spiritual pressure under which they live, never relaxing their prayer tension on heaven, rarely taking any normal diversion in too much subjective thinking. Ministers of other denominations are probably not so often the victims of this reaction.

The symptoms of such attacks in William became as familiar

to me as those of measles or whooping-cough. They were most apt to occur after what may be called long spiritual exposures—a series of "revivals," for example.

He was taken with the first one, I remember, during a six-week protracted meeting at one of his churches on the first circuit. We were spending the night with a family in the usual one-room log cabin. We occupied the company bed while our host and hostess occupied one in the opposite corner. By this time I had become resigned to this close-communion hospitality and must have slept soundly. But some time after midnight I was awakened by the deep groans of my husband.

Instantly I sat up in bed, and by the light of the moon through the window I saw his face white and ghastly and covered with sweat as if he were in mortal pain. His eyes were yawning at the dark with no real light in them. And his mouth was drawn down into Jeremiah lines of woe that are indescribable.

"William! William!" I cried aloud. "What is the matter?"

"Hush, Mary," in a tragic whisper, "don't awaken the Pratts. I have lost the witness of the Spirit. I must close the meeting tomorrow, just as the people are beginning to be interested. But it would be blasphemy to go on preaching, feeling as I do!"

"How do you feel?" I whispered, thoroughly terrified.

"As if God had forsaken me!"

I had been in it long enough to know that the "witness of the Spirit" is the hero of the Methodist itinerancy, that a preacher without it is as sounding brass and a tinkling cymbal, that he is in a role of a great play which has been rejected by the "star." I wiped the mourning dew from William's brow, laid my face against his and wept in silent sympathy. I saw something worse than disgrace staring us in the face—William deprived of his definition, William just a man like other men.

I had come of a worldly-minded family who supported the church and sustained a polite if somewhat distant relation to heaven. Religion was our relief like the Sabbath day, but it was never our state of being. And I was agreeably earthly, but I suddenly discovered that the chief fascination of William for me was that he was not earthly, that his dust was moved by strange spiritual instincts foreign to anything I had ever known. And probably nothing was further from the intention of providence when I was created than that I should become such a man's wife. But I had one enlightening qualification for the position. I loved William. I was called to that as he had been called to the ministry. And now, as I laid my face against his as the rose lies above the coffin lid, I was concerned only for William's peace.

"William," I challenged, "have you been doing wrong? Something really and truly wicked?"

"I must have," he replied with total sincerity, "but I thought I had been observing all my obligations with particular care."

"Then it's all right," I said. "God would not trifle with you about the witness of His Spirit, especially at such a time as this!"

It was not often that I showed such boundless confidence in the Lord's ways, and I was indeed far from feeling as familiar with them as I pretended. But the affectation comforted him and certainly it was no injury to the Maker of the heavens and the earth. William fell asleep at once and awakened in the proper protracted-meeting frame of mind next morning.

Many times afterward he experienced the same catastrophe, and these have been the only occasions in my life when I have put on the whole armor of God so that I might go forth properly to battle with the powers and principalities of William's darkness.

I used to wonder a great deal in those days about "the witness of the Spirit." Before my marriage I had heard little of it. I wanted to know what it was, but I never prayed for it myself. The thought occurred to me that what William called the witness of the Spirit might be the shoulder tap of his own spirit approving him now and then. But then came the deeper question. How did William come by his own spirit, that part of him which was neither flesh, nor bone, nor blood, but which had the power to make him sit up in the middle of the night to pray and to make him fast maybe all the next day?

At last I reached a comforting conclusion. That is one

peculiarity of the human, he never rests upon any other kind of conclusion. What he thinks may be so, but if it is not comforting he thinks further on into the daybreak of eternity till he gets something better, more satisfactory for his needs. This is why we shall always keep on finding God. There is something lacking in us to which God alone answers. The conclusion I came to was that we are not all called to do the same things, that William was called to preach and pray, and the witness of his spirit approved when it did right. And I was called to look after William, to see that he did not pray too much or preach too long. And I always had that sweet inward glow which he called his witness when I attended most carefully to his needs.

It may be a narrow way to look at it, but you couldn't live with William in any peace of mind without this witness of the Spirit. It would have made him unhappy to live with a person who couldn't claim it, and I've had mine these thirty years without having to pray or to fast to get it—a tender eye in me that regarded him and a heart that prayed for him.

Chapter 6

William Enters His Worldly Mind

This is the wonderful thing about the pure in heart—they do see God. And that was William's distinction. In spite of his own faults and of ethical errors in some of his preaching, he outstripped all these and did actually see God; and it made him different from other men who, however wise, do not see God. On this account I have no doubt that he fumbled more souls into the kingdom of heaven than some of the most popular tabernacle preachers of modern times.

Nevertheless, William had his worldly mind, and once he entered his worldly mind he became as naively unscrupulous as any other man of the world. Never in all the years we lived together did he repent of these particular deeds done in the body. He could be brought to repent in sackcloth and ashes for an imagined sin that he had not really committed; but no man could make him repent of a horse trade, and I never knew but one who had the best of him in one. In common with all circuit riders he had a passion for horses and a knowledge of them that would have made his fortune on the race track. This brings me to relate an incident which will serve to indicate the shrewdness and unscrupulousness of William once he took the spiritual bit in his teeth.

We were on the Beaverdam Circuit, and he had bought a new horse—a horse gifted with ungodly speed in the legs and a mettlesome, race-track temperament. On a certain Saturday after services at Beaverdam Church we were returning home in a light buggy drawn by the big, rawboned bay. When we came to a long stretch of good road William tightened the reins, took on a scandalous expression of race-track delight and let the horse out. Instantly the thin flanks of the creature tautened; he laid his tail over the dashboard, stretched his neck, flattened his ears and settled himself close to the ground in action that showed sinful training. William's expression developed into one of ecstasy that was far from spiritual, and I had much ado to keep my hat on.

Presently we heard the clatter of another horse's feet behind us, and the next moment the bay was neck and neck with Charlie Weaver's black mare. Charlie was one of the younger goats in the Beaverdam congregation whose chief distinction was that he was an outright sinner and owned the fastest horse in the county. Instantly William's whole nature changed; he was no more a minister than the red-faced young man in the buggy that was whirling giddily beside us. He tightened his reins and touched the bay with his whip. The effect was miraculous; the horse leaped forward in a splendid burst of speed. The mare showed signs of irritation and broke her gait, and the two jockeys exchanged challenging glances. At that moment we rounded a curve in the road, and in the hot dust ahead there came to view a heavy, old-fashioned carriage drawn slowly by a pair of sunburned plowhorses.

"Oh, William," I gasped, "do stop! That is the Brock carriage and this is a horse race!"

Brother Brock was a rich Methodist trustee who not only owned most of the property in the Beaverdam neighborhood,

but the church as well. He was a sharp- faced man who gave
you the impression that his immortal soul had cat whiskers. He
fattened his tyrannical nature upon the meekness of the preacher
and the helplessness of a congregation largely dependent upon
him to pay the pastor's salary and the church budget. Any
preacher who offended him was destined to be deprived of his
financial support. Knowing this I took an anxious, economical
view of the old carriage heaving forward in the road ahead and
vainly implored William to slacken his speed to a moral, ministerial gait.

In another moment it was over. The mare crashed into the
Brock's carriage on one side and the bay shattered the singletree
on the other with the front wheel of our buggy. The old plowhorses plunged feebly, then lowered their heads in native dejection, while the Brocks shrieked.

Never have I seen such a look of feline ferocity upon the
human countenance as when Brother Brock scrambled down
from his seat into the road and, with fierce intensity, added William Asbury Thompson, preacher, to Charles Jason Weaver,
loafer, drunkard and horse racer, and placed the sum of them on
the blackboard of his outer darkness.

I sat in the buggy, holding the reins over the trembling, wild-
eyed bay, while William descended and, with great dignity, tied
up the disabled singletree. There was not the slightest evidence
of moral repentance in his manner, although he expressed a
polite, man-of-the-world regret at the accident.

When Brother Brock resumed his place in the driver's seat
and Sister Brock had ascended to hers with the cacklings of a
hen who had been rudely snatched from her nest, and all the
medium-sized and little Brocks were safely bestowed beside
her, we drove on at a funeral's pace behind them. The bay was
grossly insulted, but it was the only mark of humility left within
our reach. Three days later the presiding elder[1] appeared at the

1 The presiding elder refers to a position comparable to today's district
   superintendent.

parsonage door. He was a big man, riding a handsome gray horse and wearing a look of executive severity. I trembled with apprehension, for we had heard, of course, that Brother Brock had written to him preferring charges against William for horse racing. But now I had an astonishing and unexpected view of William's character. His worldly mood was still upon him. He hurried out to meet Doctor Betterled, the elder, and, having thrown the saddlebags of his guest across his shoulder, stood apparently transfixed with admiration before the gray horse.

"I'd almost be willing to swap my bay for him!" I heard him say.

"Let's see the bay," replied Doctor Betterled guardedly.

Five minutes later, peeping through the kitchen window, I saw the spirited bay standing beside the big-headed, thick-necked gray. The two men, each with one foot planted far forward after the manner of traders, faced one another with concert eloquence concerning the respective merits of the two animals. Presently they entered the house together, Doctor Betterled evidently in a cheerful frame of mind and William wearing his chastened look.

Late in the afternoon when our guest rode away he was mounted on the bay, and he had not mentioned the horse race of the previous Saturday. William stood, the genial host, bareheaded at the gate till the rider's back was turned; then he came into the house, dropped into a chair at the open window and fixed his eyes, with a deep frown above them, upon the gray horse asleep in his dotage under the apple tree in the barnyard.

"That horse has three swollen joints, he is weak in both shoulders and I think he has a gravel in one of his forefeet!" he remarked in a tone of deep dejection.

I laughed and felt more nearly kin to him morally than I had ever felt before. There was a squint-eyed shrewdness in the way he involved and disposed of the presiding elder that was wittily familiar to me, and all the more diverting because William never suspected the Machiavellian character of his conduct. He kept his eye on God as usual, letting not his soul's right hand know what his left one was doing.

But, going back to Brother Brock and the subject of Methodist trustees in general. The preacher soon discovers that the rich ones are the most obstreperous. And besides the good ones, the rich, obstreperous ones are divided into two classes. The first class consists of those who threaten to resign if everything is not done according to their desires, which they hide and compel you to find out the best way you can. Occasionally a preacher gets into a community where everybody in the church—from the janitor to the steward and treasurer—has this mania for threatening to resign.

I shall never forget William's first experience with such a church. It was in a little village where human interest consisted in everybody hating, suspecting or despising everyone else. He went about like a damned soul, trying to restore peace and brotherly love. But they would have none of either.

Each trustee approached him privately and tendered his resignation, giving reasons that reflected upon the character of some other trustee. Then the organist tendered her resignation because the Sunday school superintendent had criticized her playing, and she retaliated by reflecting upon his unmarried morals. When the superintendent heard of her complaint and withdrawal he at once sent in his resignation, because he did not wish to cause contention in the church.

William afterward discovered that they treated every new preacher the same way, taking advantage of the opportunity to damage each other as much as possible and to try his faith to the limit. But the delightful thing about William was that where his patience and faith gave out his natural human blood began to boil, and when that started he could preach some of the finest, fiercest, most truthful gospel I have ever heard from any preacher. So it happened in this church.

When he was in certain spiritual—or, to be more precise, unspiritual—moods he refused to shave and wore the stubble on his chin, either by way of mourning or defiance, as the case might be. On this Sabbath he presented a ferocious chin to the congregation, after having waited patiently for all of the resigners to take their respective prominent pews in it. He preached a short sermon with the air of a plagued, unkempt angel; then he took up the resignation and read them out exactly as he read the church letters of new members, accepting each one and giving the reasons why. It was the most sensational service ever held in that church.

In the first place, to accept their resignations was an unprecedented proceeding and the last thing they had expected him to do. The custom had been for the preacher to persuade them to keep their offices, which they had done from year to year with an air of proud reluctance. But the sensation was when he stated, literally, what each had said of the other—calling no names, of course—and saying that he was glad that these sinners had the humility to give up positions of trust and honor in the church which they were evidently unfit to fill. He hoped before the end of the year they would be restored spiritually and worthy to perform the services they had formerly performed.

Meanwhile, there was nothing left for him to do but to appoint a committee of sinners to attend to the trustees' duties until these should be reclaimed from their backslidden state. He appointed half a dozen young men who roosted on the back benches after the manner of happy, young lost souls. I do not know whether it was astonishment or mischief that led them to accept with such alacrity the obligations imposed upon them. But William has always claimed since that they were the most active and effective trustees he ever had, that it was the first year he had ever received his salary in full, and the congregation was thoroughly cured of the resignation habit.

The second class of obstreperous trustees is easier to manage. The quality of their perversity is exactly that of the mule's. William never had to move a church, get a new roof on one or an organ for it, or even a communion table, that some well-to-do trustee did not rear back in the traces, lay back his official ears and begin to balk and kick mule-fashion.

The only way to manage them is to wait till they change their minds, just as the driver must wait upon his stubborn donkey. For you can never move one by reason or by threats. He would die and go to the wrong place rather than give up his point. This is why you will see some churches going to ruin, antiquated and out of touch with the life about them. Look inside and you will find some old mule of a trustee stalled in the Amen Corner, with his ears laid back at the preacher or at the other trustees.

I pass, without giving details, over several years; they were much like these first ones. I soon learned, however, that life in the Methodist Church was all uphill or downhill at a brisk spiritual canter. In these days it is nearly as easy to be a Methodist as it is to be an Episcopalian.

One rarely sees now the hallelujah end of a human emotion in a Methodist church. Recently, when an old-fashioned saint gave way and scandalized the preacher by shouting in one of our fashionable city churches, the trustees took her out, put her in an ambulance and sent her to the hospital. And I am not saying that the dear old soul didn't need a few drops of aromatic spirits of ammonia; but if every man who shouts at a political rally were sent to the hospital for treatment the truly sick would be obliged to move out to give them room. As for me, I contend that a little shouting is good for the soul; it is the human hysteria of a very high form of happiness, more edifying to unhappy sinners than the refrigerated manners of some modern saints.

Anyhow, I say there were no level grounds in Methodist experience in William's and my early days in the itinerancy. No matter how young or old or respectable they might be, those received into membership were expected to show signs of awful conviction for sin, to repent definitely —preferably in solemn abasement at the church altar—and to experience a sky-blue conversion.

There were no such things as we see now—boys and girls simply graduating into church membership from the Sunday school senior or junior class. I am not saying it is wrong, you understand; on the contrary, it would be much better for the church if it did more spiritual hospital work among the kind of people who are too bad even to go to Sunday school. I think they all ought to be taken into the church and kept there till they get well spiritually and decent morally. Then they might be discharged as other cured people are, to go back into the world to do the world's work properly instead of improperly.

As it is, one trouble with all the churches is that they have too many incurable saints in them, men and women who pray too much and do too little, who cannot forget their own selfish salvation enough to look after other people's without feeling their own spiritual pulse all the time they are doing it. Of late I've sometimes suspected that it is nearly as debilitating to stay in the church all the time as it would be to stay in a hospital all the time.

But I am telling now how things were twenty-five and thirty years ago. After conversion an honest Methodist's life was divided into two parts—the seasons when he was "in grace" and the seasons when he was out of it. Naturally, the preacher had his hands full looking after such members instead of having his hands full, as he does now, attending committee meetings and mission classes and what not for the ethical uplifting of the native poor and the foreign heathen. For if old Brother Settles of Raburn Gap Church was up and coming, resisting temptation and growing like Jonah's gourd spiritually, likely as not young Brother Jimmy Trotter of Bee Creek Church had backslid and gone on a spree.

There was never a night when William's family prayer instinct did not include both of them with equal anxiety, and often he would reach back into past circuits for some especially dear sinner and remind the Lord to have mercy on him also while He was at His mercies. He could forget the saints he had known, easy enough, but he clung year after year to the sinners he had found, name by name.

If the redeemed really do wear crowns in heaven, with jewels in them to represent the souls they have helped to save, I know William's will not look very handsome. There will be no flashing diamonds or emeralds in it, but he will have it set with very common stones to symbolize the kind of souls that were most dear to him. There will be a dull jade for the young country woman that he brought back home from the city and saved from a life of sin, and maybe a bit of red glass for Sammy Peters, the young man with whom he was wont to go through such orgies of repentance because of Sammy's many scandalous transgressions. And he will have a piece of granite beaten down into fine gold for the old man who repented before it was too late. And I reckon he will be sitting somewhere upon the dimmer outskirts of paradise most of the time, with grandly folded wings, holding the thing in his hands instead of wearing it on his head.

Always the people we served were poor, and, of course, we were a trifle poorer. The circuit rider is not only a priest to his people, but he is a good deal of a beggar besides. William rarely returned from an appointment or from visiting among his flock that he did not bring with him some largess of their kindness. This made pastoral visiting an amiable form of foraging and had its effect on character.

We were continually struggling against the beggar instinct that is dormant in every hopelessly poor man. We were tempted within and without. Sometimes we could not live on the salary paid, neither could we refuse the gifts offered without giving offense. If it was winter he would come back with the pockets of his overcoat stuffed with sausage, or there would be a tray of backbone, souse and spareribs under the buggy seat. If it was summer the back seat would be filled with fruit. One old lady on the Raburn Gap Circuit, famous for her stinginess, never varied her gift with the seasons. It was always dried peaches with the skins on them. But as a rule we received the very best they had to give and with a fragrant openheartedness that sweetens memory. This is the glory of the itinerancy, if the preacher sees the worst of the people, knows their faults and weaknesses better than any other man, he also knows their virtues better.

Once when we were far up in the foothills of the Blue Ridge Mountains, where the people had no money at all except that which they received for a few loads of tanbark and with which they paid their taxes, we came to desperate straits. Now it so happened that year that the women in a rich city church sent out Christmas boxes containing clothing and other necessities. We were fortunate enough to receive one of these, and I came out in singularly fashionable garments for a season, while William made a splendid appearance in the cast-off dinner suit of a certain rich but wicked congressman. The swaggering cut of the coat, however, gave almost a sacrilegious grace to his gestures in the pulpit.

Chapter 7

The Little Itinerant—And Others

On this circuit, in a house nearly as open as a barn, on a freezing winter night, our baby was born. The gaunt, dark room, the roaring fire upon the wide hearth, the ugly little kettle of herb tea steaming on the live coals, and the old mountain midwife, bending with her repulsive scroll face over me, are all a part of the memory of an immortal pain. At the end of a dreadful day she had turned with some contempt from the fine lady on the bed, who could not give birth to her child, and said simply, as if with the saying she washed her hands of the whole matter, "She ain't doin' right. I reckon somethin' is wrong."

William had ridden forth in the driving storm of snow and ice for the doctor who lived ten miles distant across the mountain. And then the hours came and sat around the bed of suffering and would not pass, nor let even midnight come. Now and again the old unsightly face peered down at me with an expression of extreme terror. The firelight made a red mist over the dark walls and the steam of the herbs filled my nostrils with a sickening odor.

At last there was an end of endurance; the hours lifted their leaden wings and hurried away; the old midwife changed to a dragon-faced butterfly, and I knew no more till the dawn and the snow spread a pale light over the world outside. The fires still blazed within, but the herb kettle was gone and the ring of ghost coals lay whitening in their ashes where it spouted and steamed; the old hag sat asleep in the chimney corner, with her hands hanging down, her head thrown back and her warped mouth gaping wide at the rafters above.

Over a little table by the door a fine white tablecloth was spread. I wondered at it dimly and what it concealed. I felt William's shaggy head bowed upon the bed and a peace in my body akin to the peace of death. Laboriously my eyes traveled back to the fine white cloth over the table. I knew all about it but could not remember. Nothing in the world mattered to me but that, whatever it was, under the cloth on the table. Presently, soft as a shade returns, it came to me, and I knew the little shape, barely curving the cloth, was my baby. Grief was an emotion I had not the strength to afford. I closed my eyes and felt tears press through the lids, and then a gruff voice sounded close to me on the other side of the bed, "Thank God!"

Opening my eyes again with a great effort and looking up I beheld him, the old, burly country doctor bending above me with his warm fingers on my wrist. But now a great emergency confronted me. My guardian angel, who has never ceased to be very high-church, urged me to meet this emergency.

"William, William," I whispered and felt his kiss answer me, "he must be baptized!"

"But he is dead, my darling!" he replied.

"Not really dead, William; he must be alive somewhere or I cannot bear it, and I cannot have him going where he will be unbaptized."

So it was done, the doctor, the old woman and William standing around the little bier, and William saying the holy words himself. And there, high up on the mountain under the very eave of heaven, swinging deep in his brown cradle of earth, the mother angels will find him, the little itinerant, with his dust properly baptized, when they come on the last day to awaken and gather up those very least babies who died so soon they will not understand the resurrection call when they hear it.

After that we took more interest in the children. They seemed real to us and nearer, whereas before they had simply passed in and out before us like little irresponsible figureheads of the future, with whom some other preacher would contend later. We never asked why they were invariably the first to come to the altar when invitations were extended to sinners during revival season. But it was curious the way the innocent little things invariably came there—no matter how awful and accusing the invitation would be—to those "dead in trespasses and sins, who felt themselves lost and undone."

So we began to be aware of the children as of strange, young misguided angels in our midst, and it was a rigid test of the genuineness of William's character that they loved him. Whenever I have seen a particularly good person whom children avoided I have always known that there was something rancid about his piety, something corrupt in his mercy-seat faculties. They are not higher critics, children are not, but they are infallible natural critics.

This brings me to tell of some of William's heavenly-mindedness in dealing with them. We were on a mountain circuit, the parsonage was in a little village, but there was no Sunday school there, nor in any of his churches. The people were poor and listless.

The children knew nothing of happy anticipations and, as is so often the case with the very poor, they sustained only the barest natural relations to their elders. There were no tender intimacies. They were really as wild as young rabbits. If we met one in the road by chance and he did not take literally to his heels, we could see him running in his spirit. We discovered that none of them had ever even heard of Santa Claus, although most of them confessed to a reluctant biblical acquaintance with

Adam and Eve.

The thought of little children passing through the Christmas season without some kind of innocent faith in the old saint took hold of William's bereaved paternal instinct. He did not mind their being bare-footed in the cold winter weather, but to be so desolate of faith as never to have hoped even in Santa Claus moved him to desperation.

A week before Christmas he visited more than a score of families and carried the news with him to every child he could find in the mountains that there was a Santa Claus, and that Santa had discovered them and would surely bring something to them if they hung up their stockings. He enlarged, out of all proportion to his financial capacity, upon the generosity of the coming saint. But when you have never had anything good in your stocking it is hard to conceive of it in advance; so the children received his confidences with apathy and silence.

Never have I seen William so industrious and so much the beggar. He beseeched the merchants in the village for gifts for his children. He had old women, who had not thought a frivolous thought in fifty years, teetering over dressing doll babies. He shamed the stingiest man in the town into giving him a flour sack full of the most disgraceful-looking candy I ever saw.

"William!" I exclaimed when he brought home this last trophy, "you will kill them."

"But," he replied, "for one little hour they will be happy and the next time I tell them anything, though it should be compound Scriptures, they will believe me."

The distribution of gifts was made very secretly some days beforehand. We climbed mountain roads in all directions to little brown cabins, leaving mysterious bags and parcels with lonesome-looking mother-women.

In one cabin, on top of what was known as Crow's Mountain, we found a handsome, healthy boy, four months old, clad in a stocking leg and the sleeve of an old coat that had been cunningly cut and sewed to fit him as close as a squirrel's skin. In another place William discovered a boy of seven who declined to believe or even to hope in Santa Claus. He was thin, with sad, hungry eyes, ragged and barefooted as usual. He had no animation; he simply could not summon enough energy to believe in the incredible.

I shall never forget this child's face. The Sabbath after Christmas we had a voluntary Sunday school on our hands. A score of odd-looking little boy and girl caterpillars appeared at church, excited, mysteriously curious, like queer young creatures who have experienced a miracle.

They entered immediately into full fellowship with William. They loved him with a kind of wide-eyed stolidity that would have tried the nerves of some people. They were prepared to believe anything he said to the uttermost. Only once was there any symptom of higher criticism. This was a certain Sabbath morning in the Sunday school when William told the story of the forty and two children who were devoured by two she-bears because they had made fun of a bald- headed man.

"I don't believe that tale!" was the astounding, irreverent comment. It proceeded from the same incipient agnostic who could not believe in Santa Claus.

"Why?" William was indiscreet enough to ask.

"Because if only two bears had eaten that many children it would have busted 'em wide open."

No one smiled. William faced five little grimy-faced boys on the bench before him, showing wide, unblinking eyes turned up in coldly rational, questioning stares, with a figuratively bulging she-bear in the eyes of each, and it was too much for him.

"We will pass on to the next verse," he announced, leaving the bear-expositor mystified, but in stubborn possession of his convictions.

Sometimes in these latter years, when things went hard with us, there would come a flash of memory and William and I would see the face of some child always as if the sun were shining on it, looking at us, believing in us from far down the years. And it has helped, often more than the recollection of older, wiser saints. Our experience was that the faces of the children we had known lasted better in memory than those of older people. And they always look right, as if God had just made them.

It was always nip and tuck in the records of William's ministry, whether he would perform more marriage ceremonies or preach more funerals. Some years the weddings would have it. Then again, the dead got the better of it. As a rule, the poorer the people we served the more weddings we helped to celebrate, and if the heroes and heroines of them did not live happily ever after, at least they lived together.

There is no hour of the day or night that William has not sanctified with somebody's marriage vows. Once, about two o'clock in the morning, there was a furious rap at the door of the parsonage. William stuck his head out of the window overhead and beheld a red-faced young farmer standing in the moonlight, holding the hand of his sweetheart, who was looking up at him with the expression that a white rose wears in a storm.

"Come down and tie us, Parson," called the groom. "You ain't got time to dress. They air after us hot-footed."

William slipped on his longtailed coat over his pajamas, hurried downstairs and married them there in the moonlight, after having examined the license the young man handed in through the parlor window. And he looked well enough from the sill up, but from the sill down I doubt if his costume would have passed muster.

Fortunately, no one thought of divorces in those days. Women stayed with their husbands at the sacrifice of self-respect and everything else save honor. And they were better women, more respected than those who kick up so much divorce dust in society nowadays. Part of their dissatisfaction comes from bad temper and bad training, and a good deal of it comes from getting foolish notions out of books about the way husbands do or do not love their wives. It seems they can't be satisfied how they do it or how they don't do it. But back there William and I never had any biological doubts about the nature of love, and the people he married to one another did not have any either.

Once I remember a bridegroom who blushingly confessed that he was too poor to pay the fee usually offered the preacher.

"But I'll pay you, Parson," he whispered as he swung his bride up behind him upon his horse; "I'll pay as soon as I'm able."

Ten years passed and William was sent back to the same circuit. One day, as he was on his way to an appointment, he met a man and a woman in a buggy. The woman had a baby at her breast, and the bottom of the buggy looked like a human bird nest, it was so full of young, tow-headed children.

"Hold on!" said the man, pulling up his horse; "ain't this Brother Thompson?"

"Yes."

"Well, here's ten dollars I owe you."

"What for?" demanded William, holding back from the extended hand with the fluttering bill in it.

"You don't remember it, I reckon, but you married us ten years ago. I was so poor at the time I couldn't pay you for the greatest service one man ever done another. We ain't prospered since in nothing except babies, or I'd be handin' you a hundred instead of ten."

I have never heard a man compliment his wife since then that I do not instinctively compare it with the compliment this mountain farmer paid his wife that day. I never hear the love of a man for his wife misnamed by the new, disillusioned thinkers of our times that I do not recall the charming testimony of this husband against the injustice and indecency of their views.

Chapter 8

I Hold The Stage

So far, the circuit rider has been the hero of these letters, but in this one his wife shall be the heroine, behind the throne at least, for scarcely any other woman looks or feels less like one in the open.

The Methodist ministry is singularly devastating in some ways upon the women who are connected with it by marriage. For one thing it tends to destroy their aesthetic sensibilities. Very often they lack the good taste of thrift in poverty, not so much because of the poverty but because they never get settled long enough to develop the hen-nesting instinct and house-pride that is dormant in us all. They simply make a shift of things till the next conference meets, when they will be moved to another parsonage.

A woman has not the heart to plant annuals, much less perennials, under such circumstances. Let the Parsonage Aid Society do it, if it must be done. And the Parsonage Aid Society does do it. You will see in many Methodist preachers' front yards fiercely-thorny, old-lady-faced roses—the kind that thrive without attention—planted always by the president of the Parsonage Aid Society. And it may be there will be a lilac bush in the background, not that the Parsonage Aid Society is partial to this flower, but because it is not easily killed by neglect. They choose the hardiest, ugliest known shrubs for the parsonage yard because they survive the best.

On every circuit, in every charge, you will find the Parsonage Aid Society a band of faithful, fretful, good housekeepers who worry and wrangle over furnishing the parsonage as they worried and wrangled when they were little girls over their communal "playhouses." The effects in the parsonage are not harmonious, of course. As a rule every piece of furniture in it clashes with every other piece, each having been contributed by rival women or rival committees in the society.

And this has its deadening effect upon the preacher's wife's taste, else she would go mad, living in a house where, say, there is a strip of worn church- aisle carpet down the hall—bought at a bargain by the thrifty Aid Society—a cherry-colored folding bed in the parlor along with a golden oak table, a homemade bookcase, four different kinds of chairs, a patent-medicine calendar on the wall and a rag carpet on the floor, with a flowered washbowl and a pitcher on a plain table in the corner, confessing that, after all it is not a parlor, but the presiding elder's bedroom when he comes to hold "quarterly meeting." Still, if I had anything to do with the new-monument- raising business in this country I would have a colossal statue raised to the living women of the Methodist Parsonage Aid Societies.

But the worst effect of the itinerancy upon its ministers' wives is the evil information they must receive about other people. If I had to select the woman in all the world best informed about the faults, sins and weaknesses of mankind I should not choose the sophisticated woman of the world, but I should point without hesitation to the little, pale, still-faced Methodist preacher's wife. The pallor is the pallor of hardship, often of the lack of the right kind of nourishment, but the stillness is not the result of inward personal calm and peace. It is the shut-door face of a woman who knows all about everybody she meets with that thin little smile and quiet eye. The reason for this is that the preacher's wife is the vat for receiving all the circuit scandal actually intended for her husband's ears.

The most conscienceless gossips in this world are to be found always among the thoroughly-upright, meanly-impeccable members of any and every church. They are the scribes and Pharisees[1] who contribute most to the building of fine houses of worship; they give most to its causes. They are the "right hands" of all the preachers from their youth up. They have never been truthful sinners. They were the pale, pious little boys and girls who behaved and who graduated from the Sunday schools long ago without ever being converted to the church. And there you see them, the fat, duty-doing, self-satisfied "firsts" in this world, who shall be last and least in the world to come.

Those least inclined to tattle about their neighbors, I found, were poor, pathetic sinners with damaged reputations, who could not afford to talk about others. They belonged humbly to the church but never figured loudly in it. And if God is God, as I do firmly believe in spite of all I have heard to the contrary, there will be something "doing" in heaven when these saint-pecked sinners are all herded in. They will wear the holy seal of His tender forgiveness through all eternity and get most of the high offices in paradise, just as a matter of simple justice.

What I have suffered morally from these vicious gossips cannot be put into words. Within a week of our arrival on a new work one of them would be sure to call. There was Sister Weekly, for example, on the Gourdville Circuit, and the parsonage here was in the little village of Gourdville. William was out making his first pastoral visits when there came a gentle knock at the door. I untied my kitchen apron, smoothed my hair, sighed—for I knew from past experience it would be the

---

1   Scribes were experts in the study of the law of Moses, while Pharisees were a sect of scribes who tried to master the test of the law in every detail and to carry out the teachings meticulously.

church's arch gossip—and opened the door. A round old lady tied up in a sanctified black widow's bonnet stood on the step.

"I am Mrs. Weekly," she explained, "and I reckon you are Sister Thompson, the new preacher's wife. Both my sons are trustees. And I thought I'd come over and get acquainted and give you a few p'inters. It's so hard for a stranger in a strange place to know which is which."

"I am glad to see you. Won't you come in?" I said pleasantly.

She settled herself in the rocker before the fire in our front room, looked down at the rug and exclaimed:

"My! Ain't this rug greasy! Our last pastor's wife was a dreadful careless housekeeper."

She had a white, seamless face, sad, prayerful blue eyes too large for the sockets, a tiny nose that she had somehow managed to bring along with her unchanged from a frivolous girlhood and a quaint old hymnal mouth. Looking up from the rug she took on an expression of pure and undefiled piety and began in the strident, cackling tones of an egg-laying hen.

"Your husband's goin' to have an awful hard time here, Sister Thompson. The church is split wide open about the organ. Old man Walker wants it on the right-hand side of the pulpit, and my sons have put it on the left-hand side, where the light is good and the choir can see the music better. It ain't decent the way Walker makes himself prominent in the church, nohow. They say he killed a man in Virginia before he came here. I might as well tell you, for you are bound to hear it anyhow. My sons say they are going to pull out and go to the Presbyterian church if Walker don't quit carryin' on so about the organ. Their father was Presbyterian, and I wouldn't be surprised if it cropped out in them. But it'll be bad for our church if they do. They pay half of the preacher's salary, and Walker scarcely pays at all. Seems to me he ought to keep his mouth shut.

"And Richard Brown has took the homestead law to keep from paying his debts. Now maybe he'll drop behind in his pledge, too. He was a right smart help in the church, though I never thought much of him morally. They say he both drinks and cusses when he goes off to Augusta. And it's a plumb shame that his wife's president of the Woman's Foreign Missionary Society. She's all right now, I reckon, but folks talked about her when she was a girl." She paused to get her second wind, folded her hands as if in prayer, turned her divine old eyes up to the ceiling and continued.

"But the Epworth League is the worst. I've always had my doubts about it. 'T won't do to git too many young folks together in a bunch. I don't care how religious they are, they'll just bust up and turn natural if you git too many of 'em together. That's what's happened here. The Epworth League kept on flourishin' so, we didn't understand it. It met every Saturday night as prayerful and punctual as clocks. But as soon as the old folks left they shet the doors, and then they'd dance like sin—been doing it for months before anybody found out. Oh! I'll tell you everything is on the downward road in this church, and your husband is going to have his hands full even if he don't starve to death!"

Every preacher's wife is the victim of such women. If she is supernaturally wise she does not handicap her husband by repeating their gossip to him. Personally, I prayed more earnestly to be delivered from this particular temptation than from any other. But never once was the Lord able to do it. Sooner or later I invariably told William every word of scandal I heard.

He never served but one church where the people in it did not "talk" about one another. I will call the place Celestial Bells, although that is not the real name of it.

The congregation was a small one, composed of well-bred, worldly-minded folk. They all danced a little, went to the theater often, wore golden ornaments and otherwise perjured themselves in the light of the membership vows in our church *Discipline*. What I wonder is, will the good, patient God—who knows that since the days of David we have had dancing dust in us, who has Himself endowed us so abundantly with the dramatic instinct, who even hid His gold about with which we bedeck and enrich ourselves—will He, I say, damn those honest, world-loving, church-giving people most, or will He take it out of the religious topknots of the church who tempted them with these "rules" in the *Discipline*?

Poor William had a scandalous time at that place readjusting his moral focus so that it would rest upon his people. Sister C and Sister Z were admirable wives and mothers. He had never had more intelligently helpful women in his congregation. That is to say, they were patiently faithful in their attendance upon its services, they professed often to be "benefited" by his sermons, they brought up their children in a new kind of nurture and admonition of the Lord; but if he went to pay them a pastoral call and have prayers with them, likely as not he would find that they had gone to take the children to the matinee.

And Brother A and Brother B were the best trustees he ever had, but they would do anything from wearing a tuxedo to going to a circus. I can never forget Brother B's prayers. Although he was modest and retiring to the point of shyness he was one of the few members in the church at Celestial Bells who could be depended upon to lead in prayer. This was frequently William's experience. More often than not the brother who could slap him on the back or sing a bass in the choir that made the chandeliers rattle would turn pale and fall into a panic if he was called on to pray. Somehow one got the notion that he felt his voice would not carry in that direction. But Brother B could open his heart at once in prayer and do it so naturally every one of us felt that we were ourselves uttering the same prayer. He never ornamented his petitions with any high-sounding phrases. He was not so much a man carrying on in a loud voice before his Maker as he was a little boy with a sore toe and troubles pertaining to his littleness and inexperience and faults and forgetfulness, all of which he let out with the emotion of a child to his father and with such reality of detail that the whole congregation accompanied him with his lamentations and regrets. Whenever I lifted my head after one of Brother B's prayers I felt better, like a child who has taken some great elder person into its confidence.

While I am on this subject of prayer, I must not forget an incident connected with Brother A. He was the most belligerent-looking peaceful man I ever saw. His brows were black and so thick they amounted to whiskers above his large, pale blue eyes. He wore a military moustache of the same color and preferred to talk through his teeth. And aside from being very prosperous and a good friend, his distinction was that he knew how to do the will of his Father with as much directness and dispatch as if it had been an ordinary business proposition.

If William wanted the church moved off a side street in a hollow, Brother A was the man who could drag it a quarter of a mile and set it on a hill, yoked up, of course, with as many other trustees as he could get. If there was anything to be done he could do it, and in the right spirit. But he was one of God's dumb saints. He had faith and he had works, but he couldn't pray, that is, not in public. This led to the incident to which I have already referred.

We had just come to Celestial Bells, and seeing Brother A so active, like a pillar of cloud and fire in the church, we did not suspect his other-world muteness. William was closing his first Sunday night service. The congregation was large and in the front midst of it sat Brother A. Immediately behind him sat Brother C, a fluent and enthusiastic trustee.

I was in the Amen Corner as usual, because it is only from this vantage ground that a preacher's wife can keep her eye properly upon her husband's congregation and be able to estimate the causes and effects of his discourse. I have sometimes suspected, indeed, that better saints occupy this Amen Corner for a less excusable curiosity about the doings in the congregation.

William closed the hymn book, looked out over the blur of faces before him and said, "Brother A will lead us in prayer."

If he had suddenly struck a short circuit and let loose a flash of electricity in the house the shock would not have been more perceptible. Everybody knew that Brother A could not lead in prayer, except William who was already on his knees with his eyes closed. Every head was bowed except those of Brother A and Brother C. They were whispering over the back of the bench that separated them. The sweat was standing out on Brother A's forehead, his brows bristled with horror, while Brother C smiled calmly at him.

"Go on, C! You know I can't pray in public!" I heard him say.

"He didn't ask me, he called on you," retorted Brother C.

Thus they had it back and forth for more than a minute. Then William groaned, which added the one touch that rendered Brother A frantic. Casting a ferociously damaging look at Brother C, he nudged the lady sitting beside him and whispered, "Lead this prayer, madam, I can't!"

And she led it in a sweet high treble that must have surprised William and even the angels in heaven, if they were expecting to hear the petition in the ordinary masculine bass which is usually characteristic of such petitions.

But I was going to tell how disconcerting it was to William to serve people who were apparently religious and worldly-minded at the same time. He could not reconcile this kind of double living with his notions of piety. At least their sins lay heavily on his conscience.

One Sabbath morning in June he entered the pulpit in a Sinai mood, determined to read the church rules and to apply them severely. He began by selecting a condemnatory Psalm, took his text simply as a threat from Jeremiah in one of his bad moods, and after a severe hymn and a mournful prayer he arose, folded his spectacles and fixed his burning eyes upon the innocent faces of his congregation, which had a "What have we done?" expression on them that would have moved an angel to impatience.

"Brethren and sisters," he said after a frightful spiritual pause, "it is my duty this morning to call you back out of the far country into which you have gone, to your Father's house. I blame myself for your dreadful condition. I have not had the courage to tell you of your faults as a preacher should tell his people when he sees them wandering in the forbidden paths of worldliness and sin. I have not been a faithful shepherd to you, and doubtless the Lord will lay your sins upon my head. But this morning I am resolved to do my duty by you, no matter what it costs."

The congregation took on the expression of a child about to be laid across the parent's knee. But when he opened the *Discipline* and proceeded to read the rules, following each with solemn, almost personal applications to conditions under his very nose, in his own church, their countenances underwent a lightning change of almost happy relief. Never can I forget the naive sweetness with which those people turned up their untroubled eyes to William and received his thundering exhortations. They seemed proud of his courage—for, indeed, he nearly broke his heart condemning them—and at the same time they seemed to be bearing with him as they would bear with the eccentricities of a good and loving old father.

Sister C and Sister Z sat near the front, surrounded by their respective cherubic broods, looking up at him with tender, humorous eyes. The children, indeed, felt something alien to peace in the atmosphere. They regarded him fearfully, then turned meek, inquisitive faces to their mothers; but those two extraordinary women never blinked or blushed from start to finish, although they were deeply dyed with all the guilt William mentioned.

The one person present who received the discourse with almost vindictive signs of endorsement was Brother Billy Smithers, a man who had lived an exasperatingly regular life in the church for more than forty years. He sent up amens fervid with the heat of his furious spirit at the end of each charge and condemnation.

Chapter 9

William and the Feminine Soul

I do not know if I make you understand that all this time the years were passing—five, ten, fifteen, twenty—and in them we went together up and down and around our little world, William offering his Lord's salvation without any wisdom of words worth mentioning, yet with a wisdom as sweet, as redolent of goodness as the carnations in heaven are of paradise.

I followed after him holding up his hands, often with my own eyes blindfolded to the spiritual necessities of the situation, praying when he prayed, though many a time I could have trusted our Father to do the square thing without so much knee-anguish of the soul; and this is how at the end of so many years in the itinerancy I began to take on the look of it—that is to say, I had faded; and although I still wore little decorative fragments of my wedding finery, my clothes in general had the peculiar prayer-meeting set that is observable in the garments of every Methodist preacher's wife at this stage of her fidelity to the cause. There is something solemn and uncompromising in her waistline, something mournfully beseeching in the down-drooping folds of her skirt, and I do not know anything in Nature more pathetically honest than the way her neck comes up out of the collar and says, "Search me!"

All this is most noticeable when the circuit rider has brought her up from his country circuit to the town parsonage and the town church, where there is such a thing as style in sleeves and headgear. I should say in this connection that William did at last "rise" that much in the church. He occasionally became the pastor in a village with a salary of, at most, five hundred dollars. The wife at this time always looks like a poor little lady Rip Van Winkle in the congregation. And her husband invariably makes the better impression because all those years while she was wearying and fading he was consciously or unconsciously cultivating his powers of personality, his black-coated ministerial presence, and even the full, rich tones of his preaching voice.

But I will say for William that he was as innocent as a lamb of any carnal intentions in these improvements. He was wedded to his white neckties as the angels are to their wings, and he was by nature so fastidiously neat that if he had been a cat instead of a man he would have spent much of his time licking his paws and washing his face. Besides, like all preachers' wives I was anxious that he should look well in the pulpit, and therefore ready to sacrifice my own needs that he might buy new clothes because he must appear in the pulpit every Sunday; especially as by this time I had the feeling of not appearing even when I was present. One of the peculiar experiences of a preacher's wife is to stand in the background at the end of every Sunday morning service and see her husband lionized by the congregation.

Another thing happened as we went on, far more important than the casting of me out of the fashion of the times. This was the change in the quality of spirituality with which William had to deal in his more cultivated congregations.

I cannot tell exactly where we made the transition, but somewhere in the latter years of his ministry he stepped out of one generation into another, where the ideals of the Christian life were more intelligent but less heavenly. The things that preachers had told about God to scare the people forty years before had come up and flowered into heresies and unbelief in their children. William actually had to quit preaching about Jonah and the whale. He had an excellent sermon on the crucial moment of Jonah's repentance, with which in the early part of his ministry he often awakened the repentant consciences of his people, but when he preached the same sermon twenty years later in a suburban town the young people laughed.

For the first time he came in contact with that element in the modern church that is afflicted with spiritual invalidism. It is composed of women for the most part who are forever wanting to consult the pastor about their spiritual symptoms. They are almost without exception the victims of moral inertia and emotional heavings. Personally I have little hope of their redemption because they are too smart to be convicted of their real sins.

Back upon the old, weatherbeaten circuits we met no such examples of mock spirituality. The men and women there had too little sense and too much virtue to go through such complicated intellectual processes to deceive themselves and others; they took narrow, almost persecuting views of right and wrong. But these teething saints in the town churches had too broad-minded a way of speculating upon their very narrow moral margins and too few steadfast convictions of any sort.

The women were the worst, as I have already intimated. Many of them were in a fluid state, dissolved by their own minds; others sustained the same relation to their souls that young and playful kittens do to their tails. They were always chasing them and never really finding them. But the most dangerous of them all is the one who refuses to take up her bed and walk spiritually and who wants the preacher to assist her at every step. There is something infernal about a woman who cannot distinguish between her sentimental emotions and a spiritual ambition.

This is why, when we hear of a minister who has disgraced

himself with some female member of his flock, my sympathies are all with the preacher. I know exactly what has happened. Some sad-faced lady who has been "awakened" from a silent, cold, backslidden state by his sermons goes to see him in his church study. (They who build studies for their preachers in the back part of the church surround him with four walls of moral destruction and invite it for him. The place for a minister's study is in his own home, with his wife passing in and out, if he has female spiritual invalids calling on him.)

This lady is perfectly innocent in that she has not considered her moral responsibility to the preacher she is about to victimize. She is very modest, really and truly modest. He is a little on his guard till he discovers this. First, she tells him that she is unhappy at home, most likely has a sacrilegious husband. I have never known one who spoke well of her husband. She has been perishing spiritually for years in this cruel atmosphere, and she dwells upon it till the preacher's heart is wrung with compassion for what this delicate nature has suffered in the unhallowed surroundings of her home.

But now, she goes on, with a sweet light in her eyes, his sermons have aroused in her a desire to overcome such difficulties and to live on a higher plane. Could he give her some advice? He can. He is so full of real, honest, truthful kindness he almost wants to hold her hands while he bestows it. Nothing is further from his mind than evil. The preacher in particular must think no evil. This places him within easy reach of the morbid woman, who can do a good deal of evil before she thinks it.

After a few visits she professes a very real growth spiritually, but—she hesitates, lowers her gentle head and finally confesses that she is troubled with "temptations." She shows her angelic confidence in him by telling them, and he is deeply moved at the almost childish innocence of what she calls her temptations. No honest woman could possibly regard them as such, if the preacher only knew it. But he doesn't know it. He sees her reduced to tears over her would-be transgressions, and before he considers what he is about he has kissed the "dear child." That is the way it happens nine times out of ten, a good man damned and lost by some frail angel of his church.

A minister is always justified in suspecting the worst of a pretty woman who wants to consult him privately about her soul, whether she has sense enough to suspect herself or not.

After observing William very carefully for thirty years I reached the conclusion that the wisest preacher knows nothing about the purely feminine soul, and the less he has to do with it the better. The thing, whatever it is, is so intimately connected with her nervous system that only her Heavenly Father can locate it from day to day.

I lived with William for thirty years and had more than my share of spiritual difficulties. But I would have as soon asked him how to cut out my dress as what to do with my soul. No man's preaching benefited me more, but in so far as my soul was feminine and peculiar to me I took it as an indication that providence meant it to remain so, and I never betrayed it, not even to him.

But I could not keep other women from doing so. There was a beautiful lady in the church at Orionville who gave "Bible readings" as if they were soprano solos. She was always beautifully gowned for the occasion and had an expression of pretty, pink piety that was irresistible. She was "not happy at home" and candidly confessed it. The lack of congeniality grew out of the fact that her husband was a straightforward businessman who took no interest in her Bible readings. But he was about the only man in the church who did not. And it is only a question of time when she would have betrayed William in the second book of Samuel if I had not intervened.

She had been coming to the parsonage regularly for a month, consulting him about her "interpretation" of these Scriptures. She asked for him at the door as simply as if I had been his office boy. And William was always cheered and invigorated by her visits. He would come out of his study for tea after her departure, rubbing his hands and praising the beautiful, spiritual clearness of her mind, which he considered very remarkable in a woman.

Poor William! I never destroyed his illusions for they were always founded upon the goodness and simplicity of his own nature. But when Mrs. Billywith began to spend three afternoons of the week with him in his study, with nobody but the dead-and-gone II Samuel to chaperon them, and when William began to neglect his pastoral visiting on this account, I couldn't have felt the call to put an end to the "interpretations" stronger than I did if I had been his guardian angel. The next time she came he was out visiting the sick.

"Come right in, Mrs. Billywith," I said, leading her into the study and seating myself opposite her when she had chosen her chair. "William is out this afternoon, but possibly I can help you with the kind of interpretation you ought to do now better than he can." She stared at me with a look of proud surprise.

"You and William have spent a very profitable month, I reckon, on II Samuel; but I've been thinking that maybe you ought to have a change now and stay at home some and try to interpret your own Samuel. Your husband's given name is Sam, isn't it? He seems to me a neglected prophet, Mrs. Billywith, and needs his spiritual faculties exercised and strengthened more than William does. Besides ..."

I never finished the sentence. Mrs. Billywith rose with the look of an angel who has been outraged, floated through the open door and disappeared down the shady street. William never knew, or even suspected, why she discontinued so interesting a study, nor why he could never again induce her to give one of her beautiful Bible readings on prayer-meeting nights.

You will say, of course, that I was jealous of my husband. But I was not jealous for him only as a husband; I was even more jealous for him as the simplest, best, most saintly man I had ever known. And the preacher's wife who does not cultivate the wisdom of a serpent and as much harmlessness of the dove as will not interfere with her duty to him in protecting him from such women—whose souls are merely mortal and who are to be found in so many congregations—may have a damaged priest on her hands before she knows it. There is not a more difficult soul to restore in this world except a woman's. Ever after it sits uneasy in him. It aches and cries out in darkness even at noonday, and you have to go and do it all over again—the restoring.

Someone who understands real moral values ought to make a new set of civil laws that would apply to the worst class of criminals in society—not the poor, hungry, simple-minded rogues, the primitive murderers, but the real rotters of honor and destroyers of salvation. Then we should have a very different class of people in the penitentiaries, and not the least numerous among them would be the women who make a religion of sneaking up on the blind male side of good men without a thought of the consequences.

Chapter 10

William Becomes a Prodigal

William made but two long journeys away from home. One was to visit a brother minister, the other was a sort of involuntary excursion he made away from God in his own mind. And as the first trip led to the second I will begin with that.

There was a young man in William's class at college named Horace Pendleton, who entered the ministry with him and joined the North Georgia Conference at the same time. William had that devotion for him one often sees in a good man for just a smart one. He placed an extravagant value upon his gifts, and he was one of the heroes of our younger married years about whom he talked with affectionate blindness.

And there is no doubt that Horace Pendleton had a gift, the gift of rising the ecclesiastical ladder. You might have thought he was in the world instead of the church, he went up so fast. He had been ordained scarcely long enough to become a deacon before he was well enough known to be preaching commencement sermons at young ladies' seminaries and delivering lectures everywhere. He had that naive bravery of intelligence which enabled him to accept with dignity an invitation to lecture on any subject from "Sunshine" to the "Psychology of St. Paul."

I remember him very well in those days, a thin, long, young man with a face so narrow and tight and bright that when he talked in his high metallic voice one received the impression of light streaming in up his higher nature through a keyhole. I specify higher nature, because Pendleton never addressed himself to any other part of the spiritual anatomy. I always had the feeling when I heard him that he inflated each word, so that some of the weightiest and most ancient verbs in the Scriptures floated from his lips as lightly as if they had been the cast-off theological tail-feathers of a growing angel. His grandest thoughts (and he was as full of them as an eggshell is of egg) seemed to cut monkeyshines and make faces back at him the moment he uttered them. Personally, I never liked him. He talked too much about sacrifice and was entirely too fortunate himself. Maybe I was jealous of him.

The contrast between his career in the ministry and William's was certainly striking. He had been made a Doctor of Divinity and was filling the best churches in his conference, while William and I were still serving mountain circuits. And it was not long before none of the churches in our conference were good enough for him, so he had to be transferred to get one commensurate with his ability. I have always thought that if he had been a land agent instead of a preacher, he could have sold the whole of Alaska and the adjacent icebergs in one quadrennium.

I may as well admit that there was an invincible streak of meanness in me which prevented my admiring him, for from start to finish he was a man of impeccable reputation and undoubtedly irreproachable character, as we use those words, and I could have admired him as anything else but a preacher. It was his shockingly developed talent for worldly success that revolted me. To this day, the gospel, the real "lose-yourself-for-my-sake" gospel sounds better, more like gospel to me if it is preached by a man who is literally poor. Maybe it is because I learned to revere this trait in William.

But in every way, always William could surpass me in the dignity of love. So he went on loving Horace Pendleton. He believed that the Lord was lavish in favors to him because of his superior worth, and this accounted for his good fortune. I never interfered with any of William's idolatries; they were all credible to him.

At last the time came when he received an invitation to visit Pendleton, who was now pastor of the leading Methodist church in a flourishing city in another state. They had always kept up an occasional correspondence, and I am sure Pendleton never received finer laurels of praise than William sent him in his letters.

We were in a small town that year in the Malarial District and William's health was not good. It was early spring, before the revival season opened, and it so happened that there was some kind of political convention on hand which enabled him to secure special rates on the railroad. So one morning in April I plumed and preened him in his best clothes and sent him on his happy journey.

When he returned a week later William was a changed man. He talked with a breadth and intelligence upon many old and new subjects that I had never observed in him before. Yet it seemed to me that something great in him had faded. He was stuffed to the neck with ethics as loose-fitting morally as the sack coat of worldly-mindedness, and he did not suspect it. His very expression had changed. He looked, well, to put it as mildly as I can, William looked sophisticated. There is a Moses simplicity about goodness that has never been improved upon by the wisest ape-like expression of the smartest man that ever lived, and William's simplicity had been blurred.

"Mary," he said to me, as we sat at our evening meal the day after his return, "I must read and study more. This visit has been an eye-opener to me. I am sadly behind the times."

"Yes, William," I replied shrewdly, for I had never heard

him talk so before, "you must read and study more, for a preacher has something bigger than 'the times' on his conscience."

"What do you mean?"

"That the times are so transient, that a preacher is called to deliver a message about what is far more permanent."

"I think, Mary," he went on, assuming the reasoning air that a man always takes when he thinks he is trying to make a woman think, but when he is only trying to make her agree with what he thinks, "I think one reason why Pendleton has gotten on in the church and been of so much more service there than I have is because he has kept up with his times. He is a very learned man, and he preaches right up to the present moment. I'd scarcely have recognized some of the Scriptures as he interpreted them in the light of modern criticism and conditions."

"You are right, William, there is no doubt that Horace Pendleton has risen in the church and been of more service to the church than you have been because he knows so much better than you do how to make it worldly-minded and how to intone the gospel to the same tune. But you, William, are you going to begin to interpret the Scriptures just to suit your times and modern conditions? I thought Scriptures had nothing to do with mere 'times,' that they belonged to the everlasting order of things."

"I fear you are prejudiced against Pendleton and incapable of seeing the good in what he says. Yet he showed a great interest in me, and he talked to me very seriously about the limitations of my ministry."

"What did he say?"

"For one thing, he said I was identified with a view of God and man and the world such as no intelligent, healthy disciple of Christ after the fashion of John Wesley ever held."

"Could you tell what *his* view of God was?"

"No, I could not. That was my ignorance. I could not keep up with him. He preached a very powerful sermon from one of the best texts in the New Testament the Sunday I was there. He couldn't have done that unless he had had a very plain view of

God."

"Oh yes he could," I retorted. "You can preach a much more satisfactorily powerful sermon in a fashionable modern church if you don't see God than if you do."

Still William persisted. He began to read strange books that Pendleton had loaned him, and the more he read the gloomier he looked. His vocabulary changed. In the course of fourteen days, I remember, the word "salvation" did not pass his lips and I could have prayed as good a prayer as he prayed any night as we knelt together. Indeed, the time came when I seriously considered making him the object of special prayer on the sly, only William was so truly good I was ashamed to show this lack of confidence in him to the Lord.

Meanwhile, the Sabbath in June approached, when protracted meeting usually began, and I knew if things did not change it would be a flat failure. For William was in a state of disarray spiritually.

"I cannot think what is the matter with me," he complained late one afternoon as we sat on the parsonage steps waiting for the prayer meeting bell to ring.

"You have backslidden, William. That's what's the matter with you! You listened to the voice of Horace Pendleton till you cannot hear the voice of God. You no longer have the single eye. It has been blackened, put out!"

That was the first and last sermon I ever preached to William. It was a short one, but it brought him forward for prayers, so to speak, and for the next few days we had a terrible time at the parsonage. He was an honest man, and he was not slow to recognize his condition once it was pointed out to him.

It is not so bad to lose the "witness of the Spirit," because you can still believe in God, and presently the witness is there again, but when you begin to read books that curtail the divinity of Jesus Christ and make your Heavenly Father just a natural force in the universe, when you bud and blossom into rationalism, there is a good deal of mischief to pay.

I do not say that Pendleton went this far, but the books he

read and loaned to William did, and they unconsciously had a more profound effect upon William than they had on Pendleton because William really had a soul. (I am not saying Pendleton did not, you understand; I am an agnostic on that subject.) But to have a soul and to be without an immediate Almighty is to experience a frightful tragedy. If a man never recognizes this diviner part of himself he may live and die in the comfort or discomfort of any other mere creature. But once you realize your own immortality (I make a distinction here between the self-consciousness of immortality and the loud preaching of it that a man may do just from biblical hearsay), you are a lonesome waif in a bad storm.

This was William's fix. But I ceased to worry once he began to pray and scourge himself, and I did not interrupt the chastening. Usually, when he insisted upon fasting all day Friday I provided little intelligent temptations to food at the earliest possible moment. But this time I let him starve to his heart's content. I reckon I am a worldly-minded woman and always shall be, but I know another, higher minded man when I see one, and I have always been careful not to drag William down. Now I was equally determined that Horace Pendleton should not.

Once during this dreadful time he came out of his study and looked at me vaguely, pleadingly, as if he wanted help.

"Don't look at me that way, William," I cried, "I can't do anything but kiss you. I never did know where your God was, but you knew, and you'll just have to go back the way you came to Him. All I know for certain is that there is a God, your kind, or you could never have lived the way you have lived, nor accomplished the things you have accomplished. You couldn't have; you haven't sense enough. And for this reason you'd better not try to think your way back. If God is God, He is far beyond our little thinking. You had better feel your way to Him. It is what you call faith in your sermons!"

Something like this is what I said to him standing before him with my head on his breast, wiping the tears from my eyes. Really, a spiritually sick preacher is about the most depressing thing a woman can have in the house. And when I looked at William, pale and hollow-eyed with his mouth puckered into a penitential angle, I longed to lay Horace Pendleton across my knees and give him what he deserved for disturbing a better man's peace.

About the middle of Saturday afternoon, however, I knew that his clouds were breaking. I heard him in his study singing,

"How firm a foundation, ye saints of the Lord,

Is laid for your faith in His excellent word."

Later on, at bedtime, he chose a cheerful Psalm to read and I heard the happy rustling of his wings in the prayer he made.

The next evening had been chosen for the initial service of the protracted meeting and I remember his text, "I count all things but loss for the excellency of the knowledge of Christ Jesus my Lord: for whom I have suffered the loss of all things, and do count them but refuse, that I may win Christ and be found in Him."

I remember it because I remember William so well that evening. He fitted into it as if it were his home. The great words seemed to belong to him. They were his experience literally. They had the authority of another simple, faithful, brave life behind them besides that of St. Paul. And the people who listened knew it. If William had made a great name and fame for himself out of preaching, if he had earned fancy salaries as the pastor in rich churches it would have been different. I don't know, of course, but it seems to me in that case they might have clanged a little like sounding brass and tinkling cymbals.

He stood in the little dim pulpit, the summer evening was fading, the lamps in the church had not been lighted, and the faces of the village folk were softened, sweetened in the gentle Sabbath gloom. He drew a picture of Paul in prison at Rome, old and anticipating his end. William never knew how to use words imaginatively, therefore they used to bunch together truthfully in his sermons as if he had woven them in. And so now we had not an elegantly painted portrait of St. Paul, but we saw him, as he really was, the man who actually had counted "all things but loss for the excellency of the knowledge of Christ

Jesus"—so out of his bonds in the Spirit.

It takes a rare preacher to portray one "found in Christ." He cannot do it with the best theological vocabulary nor the finest scientific terms. But William, I cannot tell how he did it—all I know is that every time he put his sentences together they cast again the image of the Savior upon every heart before him. He stood like a man who has his hand upon the latchstring of the door of his Father's house, counting over one-by-one the things to be lost and gained there. Nothing remained but a few simple things like loving one another. He removed the world and the cares of it and set our feet in the way of life like a wise man guiding little children.

If Horace Pendleton had put all he knew into one discourse, garnished it with a thousand terms taken from the "new theology," he could not have approached the awful simplicity and the high sweetness of that sermon.

But there is one thing I must remember to tell. As long as he lived William loved and honored Horace Pendleton with perfect devotion. That is the wonderful thing about being good. You see it always, your eyes are happily closed to evil.

On the other hand, I had occasion to learn after William's death that Pendleton regarded him with good-natured derision. He thought him a stupid man bound down to the earth by a meager theology. He even wrote an obituary notice of William that must have made his guardian angel long to kick him—all a grand display to show the contrast between a preacher like himself and a foolish old stutterer like William.

Chapter 11

Finances and Fashions

It is curious what things are revealed to us as we go along. I used to wonder, because William wondered, where and in what year Paul did this or that which is recorded in Acts. I remember how William used to get down his commentaries and squint everywhere along margins for dates to discover exactly where Paul was in the spring, say, of 54 A.D. At the time it seemed strange to me that no exact record of dates was taken concerning the doings of a man who occasionally turned the world upside down as he went through it. But now it is perfectly clear.

Those who wrote never specified whether it was the first or second Sunday that Paul said thus and so at Antioch. The record was merely of the timeless truth he uttered, because Paul and the rest of them engaged in this Scripture-making and doing back there were already out of time in their consciousness. They were figures in eternity making the great journey by another calendar than ours.

Since I have been writing this poor record of William, it is not time that matters to me. I forget to tell of his years in each chapter or to describe the changes in his appearance. The things he did, the prayers he prayed, the faith he exercised, these crowd the memory—all so much alike, as one day resembles another day, and as one prayer resembles another prayer. But the dates have long since faded from my mind.

I cannot recall, for example, when his shoulders first began to stoop, nor when he ceased to go clean-shaven, nor the year it was that his hair and beard whitened, nor when the hollows deepened to stay beneath his eyes. All I remember for certain was his changeless spirit, the unconquerable courage he showed about getting ready to put off his mortality and the definite, curious vividness with which he anticipated immortality.

And in other ways I have unusual difficulty in telling here what he said and did. The activities of a minister's life differ so widely from the activities of any other life that even to set them down requires a peculiar vocabulary. One cannot find the right words even in church reports and statistics, but they must bear some great likeness to the words used in the Acts of the Apostles. I do not know how to describe them, but every man knows them when he hears them, for the language of Christianity is the one language that never changes. It gets a new translation now and then, but it is always informed with the same spirit, the same lofty pilgrim-phrases and prayer-sounding verbs. And the minister learns them because he needs them in the world where he moves.

I make an exception here of those preachers who develop a gift for church enterprise, for getting up funds for "improvements" of one sort and another. The account they give of their stewardship is not very different from that of any other businessman. And they are needed. They do the greater part toward keeping the church housed, conspicuously steepled and visible to the world that passes by. They are the preachers in every conference who are sent to work where a new church or a new parsonage is needed. And some of them have heroic records in raising funds for these purposes. I would not take a single dollar from the sum of their renown.

But this is a memorial to William, and he was not one of

these. He was really an excellent preacher and devoted pastor, but he had more spiritual intuitions than common sense about managing the practical details of the pastorate. I recognized this deficiency in him as we went along together in the itinerancy, and feeling that it was important for the presiding elder to have a good opinion of him in every way, I must have perjured myself to every one of them year by year, singing William's praises as a businessman when I knew he was as innocent of business as the angels in heaven. If he had been the kind of man I represented him to be, he would have been a sort of hallelujah cross between Daniel Webster, John D. Rockefeller and St. Paul.

I remember the genial patience with which the gray-headed elders used to listen to my Williamanic prose. But they could not have believed me, for he was never sent to a place where visible mortar and stone work had to be accomplished for the advancement of the church. And now, when it is all over, when the violets are blooming so much at home above his dear dust, I feel at last that I can afford to confess his beautiful limitations.

After you are dead it doesn't matter if you were not successful in a business way. No one has yet had the courage to memorialize his wealth on his tombstone. A dollar mark would not be appropriate there. The best epitaph proclaims simple old Scripture virtues like honesty and diligence and patience. And you will observe that when the meanest skinflint or the most disgracefully avaricious millionaire dies, his tombstone never refers to his most notorious characteristics. His friends speak not of his scandalous speculations, but of his benevolences. Thus some of the most conscienceless rogues in a generation go down to posterity with expurgated tombstones to their memory, which of course is best for posterity.

So I do not mind now admitting that William was a poor money-raiser, but he actually did have the virtues that look good recorded on his tombstone. I can even recall with a sort of tearful humor some of his efforts at practical church thinking.

For example, he entertained with naive enthusiasm a certain proposition for regulating the support of the ministry. And he would have sent it as a memorial to the General Conference of the Methodist Church, but for my interference. He had elaborated a plan by which every Methodist preacher should receive his salary on a pro rata basis as the retired ministers do, according to the funds in hand and according to their needs. It would be taken like any other conference collection, turned in like any other treasury for this purpose. But the preacher on a mountain circuit with a wife and eight children would receive twenty-five hundred dollars and the one with only a wife, even though he might be a pastor of a rich city church, would receive only a thousand dollars.

Such a distribution of income would have placed a premium upon ministerial posterity and would have been as fatal as socialism to competition for the best pulpits in the church connection. But I did not use this argument to William. He could not appreciate it. He was even capable of claiming that it proved the virtue of his proposition.

"William," I exclaimed, when he confided in me, "promise me that you will never mention this dreadful plan, not even to a trustee or to the presiding elder. It tends to socialism, communism and to church volcanics generally. Your reputation would be ruined if you were suspected of entertaining such incendiary ideas!"

He was aghast, having always regarded the very terms I used to describe his plan with righteous horror. And that was the last I ever heard of his pro rata salary system.

Still, if all the preachers in the church were as literally in earnest about living just to preach the gospel as William was, it would have been a good plan. The fact is, many ministers are not. The very gifted, highly educated pastor of a rich city church feels it, down to his spiritual bones, that his gospel is worth more than that of the simple-minded preacher on a country circuit. And most of them would have to experience something more than the "second blessing" before they could be made to see the matter differently. I do not blame them. We just can't get over being human and greedy and covetous anywhere, it seems, especially in a rich pulpit. William stood a better chance for developing the right heavenly mind in his part of the vineyard. And I ought to have been satisfied to see the way he grew in grace and in that finer, sweeter knowledge of the Lord and His ways, but I never was.

I used to think, too, that his gospel was worth more than some other preacher's who received a better salary. But it comforts me now to know that he never thought so. If William was covetous about anything it was salvation. He was never satisfied with being as good as he was. He was always longing and praying just to be a better man, more worthy of the message he had to deliver. These were kind of angelic pleasures William took in living. And there was no mortal power, no poverty or hardship that could persuade him otherwise.

He would come back from feeding some vicious sinner with his soul exhilarated. It seemed to strengthen his spirit to drive five miles through freezing winter weather to some country church to preach to a half-dozen men and women who may have only come on such a bad day with the hope of finding that the preacher failed to come, a shepherd unfaithful to his flock in a trying season. And of course if you are called to preach this is the way to be, but if you are called to be just the wife of a preacher it is different. I do not say it ought to be, but it is.

I used to get tired of being poor in spirit. There came days when I wanted to inherit the earth, the real earth, you understand. The figure of speech might have been better for my soul, but what I hankered after was something opulent and comfortable for just the human *me*. And this brings to mind an incident that happened when I was in one of these moods.

We were stationed that year at Celestial Bells, a place where, as I have already intimated, the people had some kind of happy gleam in their eyes. They were not only willing to be Christians, they were determined to be. But they were equally determined to enjoy every other good thing in sight. This led to many social occasions, afternoon teas, receptions, innocent entertainments, to no end of visiting and to a fashionableness in everybody's appearance that was scandalously fascinating to me.

Now and then I have heard some stupid stranger refer to Celestial Bells as an ugly little town, but in my memory it is spread forever in the sun, sweetly shining like a flower garden of paradise. It was there after so many years that I came in contact again with simple human gaiety, with women prettily gowned, with the charming clatter of light conversation and with the sound of music that was not always hymnal. I do not say, mind you, that I did not listen always reverently and gratefully to William's higher talk, nor that I have ever ceased to enjoy good church music, but I am confessing that in spite of long training in experience-meeting monologues and organ tunes, I was still ecstatically capable of this other kind of delight.

As the minister's wife I was asked everywhere. In all well-bred communities the preacher's wife is given the free moral agent's opportunity to draw her own line between the world and the church. If she refuses a series of invitations to teas and clubs and receptions, it is understood that she is not of the world, will have none of it, and she is left to pursue her pious way to just the church services and missionary meetings. But I refused to draw the spiritual line between tea parties and the Bible class study evening. I accepted every invitation with delight. There was nothing radically wrong, I believe, with my heavenly mind, it simply extended further down and around about than that of some others in my position.

Only one circumstance interfered with my pleasures. This was the curious sag and limpness, the color and style of my clothes. It is no mystery to me why dress fashions for women connected with the itinerancy tend to mourning shades. When you put the world out of your life you put the sweet vanity of color out. You eschew red and pink and tender sky-blues and present your bodies living sacrifices in black materials. I do not believe that God requires it. The maker of the heavens and the earth, of the green boughs and of the myriad-faced flowers must be a lover of colors. But I cannot recall ever having seen a circuit rider's wife in my life whose few garments were not pathetically dashed with this gloom of mourning darkness.

So when we came to Celestial Bells, I had a black sateen waist and a gray wool skirt still worthy to be worn to church and prayer meeting services, and a sadder blacker gown that had done service for four years upon funeral occasions and others equally as solemn, like weddings. These were all I had, except the calicos I wore at home. The result was that I must have looked like some sort of sacrilegious crow at every social function in Celestial Bells during the first few months.

But as the spring advanced I took my courage in my hands and resolved to have a blue silk dress. The material was frightfully expensive, seventy-five cents a yard in fact, to say nothing of a white lace yoke and a black velvet belt. But no bride ever contemplated her "going away" gown with more satisfaction. I pictured myself in it before I even purchased it, attending Sister Z's tea party *looking like other women!* I do not recommend this as a high ambition, but those preachers' wives in the remote places who have worn drab and poorly cut clothes for years will know how I felt. No matter how old and consecrated these wives get, they do, in their secret hearts, often long to be pretty, to look well dressed and—yes, light-hearted. The latter is so becoming to them.

It is in the itinerancy as it is in other walks of life. Just as you think you are about to get your natural heart's desire somebody slams the Bible down on it or gets an answer to prayer that spoils your pleasure in it. So it was in my case.

It was the first foreign missionary meeting of the new fiscal year, one day in March. We met at Sister MacL's house. The jonquils were in bloom, the world was fair, and out in the orchards we could see the peach trees in one mass of pink blossoms. I never felt more religious or thankful in my life, there in the little green parlor listening to the opening hymn. The roll was called, showing that we had an unusually full meeting. The minutes were read and then came a discussion concerning dues for the coming year.

All this time Sister Shaller had been presiding with her usual dignity. She was a beautiful woman, childless, and much praised for her interest in church works. She was rich and enjoyed the peculiar distinction of wearing very fashionable gowns—even to church. Upon this occasion something reserved, potential and authoritative in her manner made me nervous. I had a premonition that she was after somebody's dearest idol. And I was not left long in suspense as to whose it was.

Fixing her wide brown eyes upon us with hypnotic intensity she said she had felt moved, unaccountably moved, to tell the auxiliary that we must support a foreign female missionary this coming year. The silence that met this announcement was sad and submissive. We were already paying all the dues we could afford—this meant fifty dollars extra—and not a single one of us wanted to send the missionary except Sister Shaller.

She went on to say, in her deep alto voice, that she knew it meant sacrifice for us, but that it was by just such sacrifices that we grew in grace, and she desired to suggest the nature of the sacrifice, one that we would probably feel the most and would therefore be the most beneficial.

"Suppose each of us resolves to do without our spring gown for Easter. Oh, my sisters! We could probably send two instead of one missionary then. And we will have at the same time curbed the weakness and vanity of our female natures!"

The rich plumes in her hat trembled with the depth of her emotions, her pretty silk skirts rustled softly. But the silence continued. If she had asked for the sacrifice of any but our Easter things we could have borne it better, but probably there was not a woman in the room whose imagination had not already been cavorting under her prospective Easter bonnet. As for me, I never felt so circumvented and outraged in the whole course of my life as a preacher's wife. I had the samples in my bag at that moment and was only waiting for the adjournment of the meeting to go to the store on my way home to purchase the silk.

There is one thing we have all noticed about a silence, especially in a company of friends. If it lasts too long it gets sullen and pregnant with the animosity of unspoken thoughts. When the silence was approaching this stage, Sister MacL, who had a heart for soothing everyone, murmured in her crooning voice, "Let us take it to the Lord in prayer!"

And we were about to rise and kneel like a set of angry children before our smiling heavenly Father, when something either moral or immoral stiffened in me, and I startled even myself with these words that seemed to come of their own accord out of my mouth, "I'll do nothing of the kind!"

I was oblivious to the horrified gaze of my companions. I felt some spirit strengthen me and give me courage. I had a quick tear-blinded vision of the years behind me and of the figure I made walking always down the aisle of some church by William in my dismal black dress, or sitting at a funeral or even at a feast, always in that ugly black garment.

"Sister Shaller," I said, looking steadily at her as a child looks at another child who is trying to take some cherished plaything from it, "you can do as you please about sending that missionary. You are perfectly able to do without new Easter clothes. As for me, I have promised the Lord to dress myself better, more like a human being and less like a woman-raven, and I intend to do it. I am tired of sitting in retired corners at parties and receptions because I look as if I belonged to a funeral. It is a matter of conscience with me, just as the missionary is with you."

I never told William what I had done. It was one of those good works that he could not have measured or appreciated. And I never knew whether Sister Shaller sent her missionary or not. She was a good woman and perfectly capable of doing it. But the other women were as grateful as if I had rescued their Easter things from a thief.

This was the only place William ever served where the people of the world flocked in and filled his church. I used to think maybe it was a way they had of returning my social friendliness to them. I accepted all of their invitations I dared to accept, and they accepted all of William's. They not only crowded in to hear him preach, they were singularly amiable about coming up to the altar if he extended an invitation to penitents who were sorry for their sins. The trouble with those people was the exceedingly small number of things they would admit as sins. But it made no difference in William's exhortations as he bent above the gaily-flowered heads at his altar. It was always, "Give up every thing and follow Christ." And if he did them no good certainly he did them no harm.

Chapter 12

The Cheerful Little Dog That Led the Blind Man

The fact that I had a worldly mind was in some ways very fortunate for William. For when all is said, this is the world we live in, not the kingdom of heaven. And while I never knew any man who understood the archangelic politics of the latter place better than William did, there were constantly occurring occasions down here on the earth, between his pulpit and the post office, when this same New Jerusalem statescraft rendered him one of the most obtuse and stubborn men in creation.

It was then that I used to feel like one of those cheerful, clever little dogs we sometimes see leading a blind man through a dangerously crowded thoroughfare. It was only then that I ever had the delightful sensation of filling the star role in the great drama of life we were acting together. And it was usually a deliciously double role, for William never knew that he was led by anything but the voice of God and the scriptural wisdom of the prophets, and the man of the world in the situation who had to be corralled and brought back into the fold rarely suspected what was happening to him.

In regard to the latter I will say I think some very good people will be obliged to wait until they actually get into the kingdom of heaven before they experience the shine and illumination of a spiritual nature. I have seen many a one of this class on William's circuits, and they are about the most difficult saints of all to manage, because they could do what they conceived to be their duty and listen a lifetime to the gospel without ever catching the least hint of its real significance. The strongest sermon William could preach on "Sell all your goods and follow me" never induced a single rich man to do it. He was fortunate if such a man gave five dollars extra to foreign missions on the strength of the appeal.

The wonderful thing about William was that these facts never clouded his convictions or discouraged him. He had a faith over and above the vain pomp and show of this world. He wore clothes so old they glistened along every seam, and little thin white ties, and darned shirts, and was forever stinting himself further for the sake of some collection to which he wanted to contribute. And all these made him an embarrassingly impressive figure when he looked out over the gew-gaws of his Sunday congregation, calling upon them to sell all their goods to feed the poor or to lay down their lives for Christ or to put on the whole armor of God and present their bodies a living sacrifice, which was their reasonable service.

Maybe if he had special freedom delivering his sermon there would be a lively response of amens from the brethren. Maybe some old black-bonneted sister would slap her hands and shout a little on the side, but nobody ever did the things he told them to do. If they had, William alone could have revolutionized human society in the course of his ministry. But he was never aware of his failure. He was like a man beholding a heavenly vision, a man supping in one long dream upon the milk and honey of far off Canaan.

For this reason, as I have said, he sometimes blundered in the world about him and I had to come to the rescue.

We were stationed at Arkville, a small village with two country churches attached to make up his circuit, when this incident happened which will serve to illustrate what I mean. The congregation was composed for the most part of men and women who worked in a cotton factory and of one rich man who owned it. Brother Sears was that most ferocious thing in human shape—a just man with a shriveled soul, a narrow mind and a talent for making money. He had built the church at Arkville and he paid nearly all the budget. He was a despot, with a reputation among his employees of having mercy upon whom he would have mercy.

William never understood him. He regarded Brother Sears as being remarkably generous and capable of growing in grace. Sears accordingly flattered and honored the church with his presence every Sunday during the first six months of William's ministry.

But there came a dreadful Sabbath when William chose for his sermon the story of the rich man and Lazarus. He preached a burning denunciation of the rich man, emphasizing his great wealth and dwelling with significant and sympathetic tone of voice upon the needy condition of Lazarus lying neglected outside his gate, afflicted with sores.

Then after singing the second hymn he capped the climax by reading out in a deep, sonorous, judgmental voice, "And the rich man being in torment lifted up his eyes to Abraham in heaven and begged for a drop of water to cool his parched tongue."

As William grew older the vision of hell seemed to fade and he laid the scenes of his discourses nearer and nearer the fragrant outskirts of heaven, but he was now in his middle age and occasionally took a severely good man's obtuse pleasure in picturing the penitentiary pangs of sinners.

I shall always retain a vivid memory of that service—William standing in the little yellow pine-box pulpit with his long gray beard spread over his breast and his blue eyes shadowed with his dark thoughts of the rich man's torment. I can still see, distinctly enough to count them, the rows of sallow- faced men and women with their hacking concert cough, casting looks of livid venom at Sears sitting by the open window on the front bench, a great red- jowled man who was regarding the figure in the pulpit with such a blaze of fury one might have inferred that he had already swallowed a shovelful of live coals.

Nevertheless William went on like an inspired conflagration. There proceeded from his lips a sulphurous smoke of damaging words, with the rich man's face appearing and reappearing in the haze in a manner that was frightfully realistic. I longed to leap to my feet and exclaim, "William, stop! You are hurting Brother Sears' feelings and appealing to the worst passions in the rest of your congregation!"

But it was too late. Suddenly Sears arose and strode out of the house. Five minutes later William closed with a few leaping-flame sentences and sat down, so much carried away with the sincerity of his own performance that he had not even noticed Sears' departure.

When he discovered the sensation he had created and the enormity of his chief trustee's indignation he was far from repentant. He simply withdrew and devoted an extra hour a day to special prayer for Brother Sears. It was no use to advise him that he might as well cut off the electric current and then try to turn on the light as to pray for a man like Sears. He had a faith in prayer that no mere reasoning could obstruct or circumvent.

The nearer I come to the great answer to all prayers the more I am convinced that he was right. But in those days I almost suspected William of cheating in the claims he made for the efficacy of prayer. Thus, in the case of Brother Sears, to all appearances it was I who brought about a reconciliation by readjusting one of the little short circuits of his perverse nature.

Brother Sears was a man who loved to excel his fellow man even in the smallest things. He not only felt a first-place prominence in the little society of the village, he strove to surpass the least person in it if there was any point of competition between them. It would have been a source of mortification to him if the shoemaker had grown a larger turnip than he had grown.

After Sears had sulked for a month, William and I were walking by his garden one day and saw him standing in the midst of it with a lordly air. William would have passed him by with a sorrowful bow, but I hailed him, "Good afternoon, Brother Sears! You have a beautiful garden, but I believe our pole beans are two inches taller than yours on the cornstalk."

He was all competitive animation at once, measured the curling height of his tallest bean vine and insisted upon coming home with us to measure ours, which, thank heavens, were four inches shorter.

He was so elated over this victory that he apparently forgave William on the spot for his fiery sermon and handed him ten dollars toward his quarterly salary to indicate the return of his good will.

"Mary," said William, staring down happily at the crisp bill in his hand as Sears disappeared, "never say again that the Lord does not answer prayer!"

For a moment I felt a flash of resentment. Who was it that had had the courage to accost Sears in his own garden? Who had coaxed him all the way across town into our garden to measure our bean stalk? Who was it that had thought up this method of natural reconciliation, anyhow? Not William, walking beside us in sad New Testament silence.

Then suddenly my crest fell. After all, I was merely the instrument chosen by which William's prayers for Sears had been answered. To his faith we owed this reaction of grace, not to me, who had not uttered a single petition for the old goat.

From time to time William had queer experiences with the political element in his churches. This was composed usually not of bad men, but of men who were unyielding Democrats or Republicans. Likely as not, the leading trustee would be the manager of the political machine in that particular community.

There was Brother Miller at Hartsville, for example, a splendid square-looking man with a strong face, a steady gaze and an impeccable testimony at "experience" meetings. He held up William's hands for two years without blinking and professed the greatest benefits from his sermons. No man could pray a more open-faced, self-respecting prayer, and not one was more conscientious in the discharge of his duties to the church and the pastor. It never seemed to disturb him that the portion of the community which was opposed to the political machine that elected everything from the village coroner to the representative regarded him as the most debauched and unscrupulous politician in that part of the state. He simply accepted this as one of his crosses, bore it bravely, and went on perfecting his remarkably perfect methods for excluding all voters who did not vote for his candidate.

He would confide in William sundry temptations he had and enlist his sympathy and admiration because of the struggle he professed to have in regard to strong drink, although he never actually touched intoxicants. But never once did he mention or admit his real besetting sin. He was willing to repent of everything else, but not of his politics. St. Paul himself could not have dragged him across the Democratic party line in that county, not even if he had showed him the open doors of heaven.

I do not know what is to become of such Christians. The country is full of them, and if they cause as many panics and slumps and anxieties in the next world as they do in this one we shall have a lot more trouble there than we have been led to believe from reading Revelation.

Chapter 13

William Wrestling With Traveling Angels

I have had little to say about the joy of William, although he was one of the most joyful men I have ever known. The reason is I never understood it. His joy was not natural like mine (in so far as I had any)—it was supernatural and not at all dependent upon the actual visible circumstance about him. It used to frighten me sometimes to face the last month before quarterly conference with only two dollars, half a sack of flour and the hock end of a ham.

But it was then that William rose to the heights of a strange and almost exasperating cheerfulness. He could see where he was going more plainly. Our extremity gave him an opportunity to trust more in the miracles of providence, and that afforded him the greatest pleasure. He was never weary of putting his faith to the test. He was like a strong, wrestling Jacob going about looking for new angels to conquer. And I am bound to confess that his Lord never really failed him, although He sometimes came within five minutes of doing so.

One Sabbath, I remember, William had an appointment at a church ten miles distant where he was to begin a protracted meeting. At the last moment his horse went lame. It so happened that some weeks previous William had overreached himself in a horse trade. He had swapped an irritable crop-eared mare for a very handsome animal who proved to have a lame forefoot.

This horse would lay his tail over the dashboard and travel like inspiration for days at a time up and down the long country roads; then, suddenly, if there was a hurried message to go somewhere to comfort a dying man or preach his funeral, the creature would begin to limp as if he never expected to use but three legs again. I believe William suspected the devil had something to do with this diabolical situation, for he never gave way to impatience as an ordinary man would have done in such a predicament. Upon the occasion I have mentioned, he helped the old hypocrite back into the stable with a mildness that exasperated me as I watched with my hat on from the window, for it was already past the time when we should have started.

"Silas is too lame to travel today," William said a moment later as he entered the kitchen.

"But what will you do, William?" I exclaimed, provoked in spite of myself at his serenity. "It will be dreadful if you miss your appointment at the beginning of the meeting."

"I can do nothing but pray. Mine is the Lord's work, doubtless He will provide a way for me to get to it," he answered, withdrawing into the parlor and closing the door behind him.

I knew that meant wrestling with one of the traveling angels and held my tongue, but my anger was not so easily controlled. I flopped down in the chair, laid my head upon the window sill and yielded to tears. I was far along in my middle years then, but never to the end did I get accustomed to the stubbornness of William's faith. I always wanted to do something literal and effective myself in an emergency. I seemed to be made so that I couldn't look to God for help until I had worn myself out.

While I sat there in a sort of tearful rage over William and the horse, there was a sound of wheels at the front gate. I arose, hastily wiped my eyes, and was just in time to face William's smiling countenance in the parlor doorway.

"Mary, Sister Spindle is not well, and Brother Spindle has driven by to offer us seats in his carriage."

Brother Spindle was the only man in the community who owned a carriage and horses.

I flung my arms around William's neck and whispered, "Forgive me, William, I never can get used to it that the Lord is illogically and incredibly good to you. But I am glad to tag along after you in His mercies."

He had a gentle way of enjoying these triumphs over me. He would cast the blue beam of his eye humorously over me, and then kiss me as if I were still young and beautiful.

Never in all our married life did he get the best of me in an argument. His arguing faculty was not highly developed. It was easier to silence him that to stir him into opposing speech. But whenever he entered the sacred parsonage parlor and closed the door after him, I always knew he would have the best of me one way or another when he came out.

But it was not this faith in prayer that confused me most, it was the answers that William and others like him received to their prayers. We never went to any church where there was not at least one man or woman who knew, actually knew, how to reach his or her empty hands up to God and get them filled. And they were always people of rare dignity in the community, although some of them bordered on the simplicity of childhood mentality.

I recall in this connection Sister Carleton. She was a very old woman who seemed to have settled down mostly below her waist. Her shoulders were thin, her bosom flat, but she widened out in the hips amazingly. Her face was the most beautifully wrinkled countenance I ever beheld. Every line seemed to enhance some celestial quality in her expression. And she had the dim look of the old after they begin to recede spiritually from the ruthlessness of mere realities. She had palsy and used to sit in the Amen Corner of the church at Eureka, gently, incessantly wagging her lovely old head beneath a little black bonnet that was tied under her chin with long black ribbons.

Sabbath after Sabbath, year after year she was always to be seen there, sweetly abstracted like an old saint in a dream. She had one thought, one purpose left in life. This was "to live to see all of my boys saved." These were three middle-aged men, all of whom had been wild in their youth. Her one connection now with the church was expressed, not by any personal interest in the preacher or his sermons, but in this thought for her children.

Sometime during every experience meeting we always knew that Sister Carleton would rise trembling to her feet, steady herself with both hands on the bench in front of her, look about vaguely and ask the prayers of "all Christian people" that her boys might repent and be saved from their sins. They were already excellent and prosperous citizens and remarkable for their devotion to her, but she was not a woman to mince matters. They had not been converted, therefore she prayed for them as if they were still dead in their trespasses and sins.

The first year of William's ministry in this place the two younger sons were converted and joined the church, but the oldest still "held out," as the saying was. In fact, he stayed out of the church literally, never coming to any service.

The next year Sister Carleton had grown very feeble, but at a consecration meeting held one afternoon before the regular revival service at night she appeared as usual. Before the closing hymn she arose, clasped her old hands over the back of the bench in front of her and made her last petition for the "prayers of all Christian people."

"Brother Thompson," she concluded in the quavering voice of extreme age, "I have prayed for my youngest boy fifty years, and for my second boy fifty-two years, and for my oldest son nearly sixty years. The two youngest air saved now, but t'other is still out of the fold. I ain't losin' faith, but I'm gittin' tired. Seems as if I couldn't hold out much longer. But I can't go till Jimmy is saved. I ain't got nothin' else keepin' me but that."

She paused, looked about her as if she felt a memory brush past. "When he was jest a little one, no higher 'an that, he was afeerd of the dark. I always had to set by him till he was asleep. And now, seems as if I couldn't leave him for good out in the dark. I want to ast you to pray, not that he may be converted, but that he may be converted this very night. I ain't got time to wait no longer—seems as if I'm jest obliged to git still and rest soon."

She sank back upon the bench, and I wondered what William would do. I never was prepared for the audacity of his faith.

"Sister Carleton," he replied, "I feel that your prayer will be answered. I've got the faith to believe your son will come here tonight and be saved from his sins."

I wished that he had not been so definite. I felt that it would have been wiser to give some general expression of hope. I feared the effects upon the rest of the congregation and upon William if we returned for the night service and James Carleton should not be there, and I was sure he would not be. I reckon first and last I must have halved the strength of William's faith by my lack of faith.

The truth is so bold, so absurd from the present worldly point of view that I almost hesitate to write it here. James Carleton *was* at the evening service. He was the first man to reach the altar when the invitation to penitents was given. He was soundly converted and lived a changed life from that hour.

The next night Sister Carleton was not in her accustomed place for the first time in nearly forty years. A month later she passed away, having already received the joy of her reward in the salvation of her children.

I have noticed that rich people do not have this kind of faith in prayer. They want, as a rule, only those things that can be bought with money, and they buy them. I have never seen a rich father nearly so anxious for the salvation of his children as he was for their success in the world. And the same thing has been my observation in regard to rich mothers. Sometimes they pray for their sons and daughters, but they do not often mean what they pray, and God knows it, for He never horrifies one of them by granting their prayer.

Still, there is a kind of sacrilegious confidence in prayer that always offended some delicacy in me, and William felt it too, only he never learned how to condemn it. His sense of reverence was not sufficiently discriminating. And there was an occasion where I had to rid him and his congregation of this sublimated form of spiritual indecency.

As I have said, we were sent to small stations, village churches, or mission churches in the factory edges of the big cities. But William's years, the hardships and anxieties, both earthly and unearthly, to which he had been exposed began to take their toll on his strength.

The year we were at Springdale as the summer came on he felt unequal to conducting the usual six-week protracted meeting without help. And while six weeks may seem a long time to hold such services, it is really a very short time for people to get revived and heaven-minded when all the rest of the year they have been otherwise-minded. The wonder to me was that men who had driven hard bargains and hated one or more neighbors for ten months, that women who had given themselves over to the littleness and lightness of a small fashionable life in a small town, or to gossip about those who did, could so quickly recover their moral and spiritual standards in a revival.

I remember that it was William's custom, as soon as there was the least interest manifested, to have a very searching service for his church members in which he called upon all those who were at enmity with one another to rectify whatever wrong they had committed and to be reconciled. Nearly always some stiff-necked trustee had had a row with somebody else, likely as not a sinner. William would be expected to go out and find the man, whoever it was, patch up the difficulty and report at the next service.

I can see now the old spiritual hard-heads in William's congregations with whom, year in and year out, he had the greatest trouble. They always managed to "fall out with somebody" between revivals. But nothing in or out of the kingdom of heaven would make one of them admit he was in the wrong or induce him to go to the other person and attempt a reconciliation.

The most you could get out of any one of them would be that if his enemy came to him and asked his pardon, he was willing to forgive him! If the said enemy was a good-natured fellow, William usually managed to get him to make this concession, otherwise the old hard-head remained cold and aggrieved throughout the revival, maybe casting a damper over the whole meeting, a figure in the Amen Corner at which the young, unregenerated sinners would point the finger of scorn and accusation when they were implored to repent and believe and behave themselves.

No one who has not been through it can understand how heartbreaking all this is to the preacher and how wearing it is on his nerves. There have been times when I should have been almost willing to see William lose patience and expend about two pages of fierce, infernal vocabulary on some old stumbling block in the church. But he never did. And it will serve them right if the ten thousand prayers he made asking God to soften their obdurate hearts are registered against them somewhere in the debit column of the Book of Life.

Thus it came to pass that William was wearing out and no longer able to get through a protracted meeting alone. So at Springdale he engaged Brother Dunn to come and help him.

Brother Dunn was what may be called a professional evangelist. We had never seen him, but he had a reputation for being "wonderfully successful" with sinners. And if sinners made a ripe harvest, Springdale was as much in need of reapers as any place we had ever been. You might have inferred that the original forbidden fruit tree flourished in the midst of it, the people were so given to frank, straightforward sinning of the most naively primitive character.

I never knew how William felt, but I was not favorably impressed with Brother Dunn when he arrived on the late evening train, a frisky, dapper young man who looked in the face as if his light was turned too high. That night as he preceded us up the aisle of the church which was crowded to hear him, he showed to my mind a sort of irreverent confidence in the grace of God.

The service that followed was indescribable in any religious language, or even in any secular language. Brother Dunn brought his own hymn books with him and distributed them in the congregation with an activity and conversational freedom that made him acquainted at once.

The hymns proved to be nursery rhymes of salvation set to what may be described as frivolous music. Anybody could sing them, and everybody did; and the more they sang the more cheerful they looked, but not repentant.

The service was composed mostly of these songs, interspersed now and then with wildly excruciating exhortations from Brother Dunn to repent and believe. He explained, with an occasional "Ha! Ha!" how easy this was to do, and there is no denying that the altar was filled with confused young people who knelt and hid their eyes and behaved with unusual reverence under the circumstances.

The cheating began when Brother Dunn attempted to make them "claim the blessing." He induced half a dozen young girls and two or three young men to "stand up and testify" that their sins had been forgiven. These were simple young creatures who had no more sense of the nature of sin or the depth of genuine repentance than field larks.

Later he frisked home with us, praising God in little foolish words and rejoicing over the success of the service. Shortly after he retired to his room we heard a great commotion punctuated with staccato shouts. William hurried to the door to inquire what the trouble was. He discovered Brother Dunn hopping about the room in his nightshirt, slapping his palms together in a religious frenzy. He declared that as he was praying by his bed a light had appeared beside him.

William tried to look cheerful and blessed, but one thing I can always say for him is that he was an honest man in dealing with the most illusive and deceptive things men have ever dealt in—that is, spiritual values—and the more he observed Brother Dunn, the more his misgivings increased.

The next morning I met the evangelist in the hall.

"Hallelujah!" he exclaimed.

"What for?" I demanded coldly.

He gave some stammering reply. But that was the beginning of the end of his spiritual peace in our house. After that I consistently punctured his ecstasies, quoting some of the sternest Scriptures I could remember to confound him.

William remonstrated with me. He said Dunn told him my lack of spirituality "depressed him."

"And, William, his lack of reverence incenses me. If you don't get rid of that cotton-haloed evangelist everybody in this town will claim a 'blessing' without repenting or being converted," I replied.

Fortunately Dunn dismissed himself. He said that it was impossible to have a revival in such an atmosphere. He implied as plainly as he could that he was sorry for William, accepted the sum of ten dollars which had been promised him for his services and left.

I have never known what to think of such preachers. No one who ever knew a man like Dunn can doubt his sincerity. But they cultivate a kind of spiritual idiocy and frenzy that is more damaging to souls than any amount of hypocrisy.

I have always been thankful that the joy of William in the religious life was a stern and great thing, no more resembling this lightness, this flippancy than integrity resembles folly.

Chapter 14

Curious Facts About The Nature of a Priest

What we call history is a sorry part of literature, confined to a few great wars and movements in national life and to the important events in the lives of a few important people. The common man has never starred his role in it. Therefore, it has never been written according to the scientific method. It is simply the spray—the big splash—humanity throws up as it goes down into the sea forever. It is what most of us do and what we think perishes with us, leaving not a record behind of the little daily deeds and wing-flappings of our spirits that really make us what we are. This is why we make so little progress. The history of the great majority is never compiled for reference. We are always bunched in a paragraph, while the rest of the chapter is given to His Excellency, the President, or some other momentary figure of the times.

Nobody knows exactly how the planters of Thomas Jefferson's day lived. We must depend upon fiction to give a sort of romantic impression of them. And fifty years from now no one will know how the farmers and brick-masons, grocers and merchants managed their affairs in our own times. We shall be obliged to accept the sensational accounts left by a few wild-eyed, virus-brained socialists.

I do not know that I ought to pretend to rescue the class to which William belonged from the same kind of oblivion. But by keeping memories of the little daily things in life a preacher's wife learns some curious facts about the nature of a priest—facts that should enable the reader to make profitable comparisons between those of the old and those of the new order, and to determine which is the real minister and which is not.

One thing I discovered was that in this life on earth you cannot domesticate a preacher like William. A woman might get married to him and hang like a kissing millstone about his neck; she might sew on his buttons, bear children for him, teach him to eat rolled oats, surround him with every evidence, privilege and obligation of strong earthly ties and a home; but he will not live there in his spirit. He belongs neither to his wife nor to his children, nor to the civilization of his times. He belongs to God, and not to a god tamed and diminished by modern thought, but to The God, the one who divided the light from darkness, who actually did create Adam and Eve and blow His breath into them, who accepted burnt offerings sometimes, and who caused flowers to bloom upon the same altars between times.

So William never really belonged in his own house with his own body, his own wife and his breakfast, though he often rested there and seemed to enjoy the latter. He was more at home in the Psalms. I will not say he went so far as Jehovah, but when he was in a Leviticus-frame-of-mind very few of the minor prophets satisfied his cravings for the awful. The gentle springtime of his heart was when he took up with Saint John in the New Testament. He never professed the intimate fellow-feeling I have heard some conceited preachers express for Saint Paul. William was not a great man; he was just a good one and too much of a gentleman to thrust himself upon a big saint like Paul even in his imagination.

I do not know which has been the greatest influence in making me what I am—the sense of reverence I had for him and his high Bible company or the sense of bereavement I had when, having fed him and warmed him, he was still "not at home" with me, but was following some pillar of cloud in his thoughts toward his great God's distant eternity.

A woman is a very poor creature. I think she hankers more for just love than she does for heaven. I don't know how she will get on in a place where there is neither marrying nor giving in marriage. It's bound to be hard on her if the Lord does not give her something more than a harp and a golden crown with which to fill the aching void she is sure to have somewhere under her breast feathers.

But no one can say that I did not stand by William through the entire widowhood of my marriage. I was the world-compass of his life, always sitting in his Amen Corner with my attention fixed anxiously upon the spiritual pulse of the congregation, always giving him the most nourishing food our limited means afforded, always standing between him and sordid dickering with the butcher and candlestick maker, always making myself a Great Wall of China to separate him on sermon-making days from the church public.

Many a time I have taken my hands out of the biscuit dough to meet a trustee who was determined to see him about the increased foreign mission apportionment, or it might be the Sunday school superintendent coming to discuss the May picnic. I could usually pacify the trustee and put off the superintendent. But if it was a messenger from some remote neighborhood on the circuit coming to say that Brother Beatem was dead, and the family wanted Brother Thompson to conduct the funeral services next morning at the nearest Methodist church, I would be obliged to give in, even if William was in the very heat of his sermon construction. For a funeral is a thing that cannot be put off. The corpse will not endure it, nor the family, either, for that matter. They want the preacher to be on hand promptly with all the laurels of language to bestow upon their dead in the funeral discourse.

And this brings me to mention a peculiarity of surviving relatives as a class. They demand that the pastor of the dead man or woman shall furnish him his titles to mansions in the sky whether he deserves them or not. Even if Brother Beatem was a mean man who neglected his wife and children, cheated his neighbors, abused his horse and failed to support the church, he must have a funeral that praised him for a saint. And if the pastor failed to do this the surviving relatives whom the dead man had victimized every day he lived would be the first to resent it.

I never knew but one pastor who told the truth in a funeral sermon, and he had to be transferred immediately by his presiding elder. The whole community regarded it as one of the most brutal outrages that had ever been perpetrated in their midst.

As for William, there was something sublime in the way he permitted his mind to skip the facts and stir his imagination when he preached a funeral. The curious part of it was that he believed what he said, and generally by the time he had finished nearly everyone else believed it, too. There were occasions, of course, when he was disgracefully duped by the surviving relatives.

However, I pass over a thousand little epitaphs of memory and come to our last years in the itinerancy. And it is curious how life winds itself into a circle, like the trail a lost man makes in the desert. After a few years as pastor of village churches, William was sent back to the country circuits. He was failing some, and of course younger and more progressive men were needed in the villages —preachers who could keep up with the committee meeting times in modern church life.

Also, I am obliged to admit William was a poor church committeeman. Occasionally he would go off to see an old sick woman or some barren fig-tree man who was not even a member of the church, and forget all about an important committee meeting on the brotherhood of man. This would give offense to some of the people in the church, who in turn would complain that he was not sufficiently interested in spreading the gospel.

As I have said before, William was a good man, but he was

neither brilliant nor enterprising as we understand these terms nowadays. He never did get it into his head that salvation could be communicated to a dying world by a thorough organization of it into committees that furnished not only the salvation, but also the whole district which had to receive this salvation as fast as it was offered. This seemed as simple as a rich man's charity, but William couldn't see it.

Somehow, he was secretly opposed to it. He was for catching every goat separately and feeding him on truth and tenderness till he turned into a lamb. It was no use to argue that this required too much time and would take an eternity to get the world ready for heaven. William refused to think of immortal souls as if they were hordes of heathen cattle that must be brought into the salvation market on the hoof as soon as possible.

As he grew older and more set in his ways, William became a trifle contrary about it, like a thorny old priest who has received private orders from his God to go on seeking his lost lambs one at a time. Once he insulted a man who came to him about the Laymen's Movement which was organized to convert the world to Christianity in this generation and probably before Christmas.

"We can do it if we have faith enough!" said he.

"No, you can't!" retorted William. "Not unless the heathens get faith enough to believe, and faith is a thing you cannot send out through the mail as if it were sample packages of patent medicine!"

Such talk as that sent him back to the circuits, where there were the same old fashions in sleeves and headgear for women, and where he could take his text from Jonah's gourd if he chose without exciting the higher critical faculties of his congregation.

It was harder on us in some ways. I never could understand why the old preachers who have gotten rheumatism in their knees, and maybe lumbago besides, should be sent back to the exposure of all kinds of weather on the circuits, while the young ones with plenty of oil in their joints could fatten in the more comfortable charges. And I am not the one to say with resignation that it is "all right." Still, the good God evens things up in wonderful ways.

William got so stiff in his legs toward the last that he had to stand up to pray; but we had come back to the region of simplicities, where there were just three elements to consider and put together in his sermons—man, his work and his God, and they were only separated by a little grass, a few stars and the creation light and darkness of days and nights. When a man gets as close to home as that, he does not mind the pains in his moral body. At least William never complained.

Looking back, I think he was at his best about the time he went back to the real circuit itinerancy. Faith, I think, gave him a halo. You could not see it, but you could feel it, and in this connection I recall an illustration of the difference between such a halo and the "aura" we hear so much about these days from people who think they are interested in psychic phenomena.

We were on a circuit which included a summer resort, and the varieties of diseases among patients in a sanitarium are as nothing compared to the mental, moral, spiritual and physical disorders to be found among the class who frequent these health spas.

To this place came a "New Thoughter" who was always in a spiritual sweat about her "astral shape." She manifested a condescending interest in the Sunday services at our church, which finally led her to call on William one afternoon at the parsonage. She was a dingy little blonde with a tight forehead and a thin nose. William was sitting alone in the peace of his spirit behind the morning glory vines on the front porch. Providence had wisely removed me to the sewing machine in the adjoining room. The sense of humor in me has never been converted, and there were occasions when it was best for me not to be too obviously present when William was examining the spiritual condition of some puzzled soul.

He had risen and seated this "New Thoughter," then sat down opposite, regarding her with a hospitable gaze. She had the fatal facility for innocuous expression common to her class. All the time I knew William was waiting like an experienced fisherman for a chance to swing his net on her side of the boat. The poor man did not dream that she was one of those unfortunate persons who has swapped her real soul for Eastern mysticism. But presently she let it out.

"Mr. Thompson," she began, without a rhetorical pause to indicate the decimal points between her thoughts, "I was interested in what you said about immortality last Sunday. Now, I wonder if you know it is an actual fact that by breathing rhythmically thirty times, counting three while you inhale, three while you exhale and three while you hold your breath, you can actually get in touch at once with your astral shape?"

William fumbled in his pocket for his glasses, deliberately put them on and then regarded her over the steel rims. I could see the Jehovah crest of his spirit erect itself as he replied with divine dignity, "Madam, I do not know what you mean by your astral shape, but I do not have to pant like a lizard to keep in touch with my soul!"

But she bore with him, showing far more calmness than he as she went on to describe the wonderful power of spirit she had developed. She had even gone so far, she said, as a matter of experiment, to "put her thought" upon the unborn child of a friend, and when the child was born it did not look like its own mother or father, but was her exact image. Now, she declared, she was sure it was her own "thought" child. And what was more convincing still, she had at last attained to a "sky-blue aura"—she added this with an indescribable air of triumph. William tightened his spectacles on his nose, drew his face close and stared at her with the sort of scandalized expression Moses must have worn the first time he caught sight of the golden calf.

"Madam," he exclaimed after a dreadful, inquisitive silence, "I can see no signs of an aura, either blue or otherwise; but if you actually did try to steal another woman's child with your thoughts you have been guilty of an unimaginable meanness, and you should go down on your knees to almighty God for forgiveness!"

William never was at his best when brought into contrast morally or intellectually with the temporary illusions of modern times. They cast him in an unbecoming light and gave him a look of the grotesque, as a great and solemn figure on a vaudeville stage suggests the comical. He belonged to a time when the scriptures of men's hearts had not suffered the moderation and sacrilege of the sense of humor.

There were occasions, indeed, when I could not preserve a proper inner reverence for his favorite hymns, as, for example, when he would be standing during a revival season behind an altar lined with "dying souls" who had come for prayer. In order to interpret for them a proper frame of mind he would sometimes choose one of Isaac Watts' famous hymns. He would stand with his feet wide apart, his fingers interlaced, palms downward, eyes lifted in anguished supplication and sing in his great organ bass:

Inspire a feeble worm to rush into Thy Kingdom, Lord,

And take it as by storm!

Still, these words do express a high form of courage, and I have seen many a "worm" rise shouting from the altar rail under their inspired meaning.

The sense of humor has, in my opinion, very little to do with poetry or salvation. It belongs entirely to the critical human faculties, and I have found it one of the greatest limitations in my own spiritual development. And as time went on I was more and more convinced that this was an evidence of a lower imaginative faculty in me rather than in William. He had less humor, but he had infinitely more of the grace that belongs to immortality. He had a spirit that withstood adversity, hardship and failure, with a sort of ancient dignity that could face tragedy with life-giving fortitude. I love best to think of him in relation to the bare and awful sorrows that show so nakedly in the lives of poor, simple folk.

I can see William now in the dismal twilight of one winter evening as he started on that strange mission to see Mrs. Martin, looking like an old, weatherbeaten angel braving a storm. The wide brim of his black hat flared up from his face in the wind, his long, gray beard was blown over the shoulders of his greatcoat. He had started without his muffler. I ran out to fetch it and, winding it about his neck, I saw the blue gleam of heaven in his eyes that always turned young when he was on his way to roll the stone away from the door of some sinner's heart.

"William," I cried, "it's going to be an awful night; don't go—she is not a member of your church."

"Nor of any other; but she is all the more in need of help," he replied, putting his foot in the stirrup to mount his horse.

Mrs. Martin was a vague little widow, superstitious about dreams, who lived with her two small children in a thickly-populated neighborhood around a stone quarry. The day before, the community had been shocked to learn from someone who happened in just in time to prevent the tragedy, for Mrs. Martin had suddenly gone insane and had tried to kill both of her children. She had to go to the asylum, of course; but pending the preliminary trial for lunacy she lay silent on her bed with staring, horrified eyes, surrounded by watchful neighbors. Suddenly toward night she had grown restless and had implored them to send for the Methodist preacher. To quiet her a messenger had come, and William made haste to go to her.

He found her sitting in the middle of her bed, her face thin and white, the very picture of misery. The moment she was alone with him she poured forth such a tale of degradation as rarely passes the lips of a woman.

Since a year after her husband's death she had been the mistress of the manager of the quarry. She had lived in the most atrocious debauchery for years; no one had suspected, and she had not suffered a qualm. But two nights before, she had gone to the bed where her two little girls lay asleep, and suddenly it had come upon her that her way of life was to be discovered now, very soon, and not by strangers, but by her own children growing old enough to observe and understand. Moreover, her degradation would become theirs. And then it came—the horror that had convinced her the only way out was to kill them and then herself. Now, what was to be done? She was not insane.

She was just a sinner who felt obliged to be damned!

God had at least a dozen ways of inspiring William and not all of them orthodox. Instead of harrowing this woman with a prayer, he took on a competent executive air.

"You are to do nothing," he told her, "and be sure you do not confess your sin to anyone else. Leave everything to me. We will see about the forgiveness later. Now you are to rest and not think till I get the way clear for you."

He went out, told the attendants that Mrs. Martin was not insane, but had suffered a shock and would now be all right. They thought he had achieved a miracle when they returned to the room and found her weeping like any other sane woman.

Before daylight William had escorted the manager of the quarry to the nearest railway station with instructions never to return, so emphatically given that he never did. William prayed earnestly for the unfortunate woman, but he forbade her to pray for herself until long afterward, when she had resumed existence upon the simple basis of being the innocent mother of her innocent children.

"If she begins to agonize in prayer," he explained to me, "she will go mad again. As soon as she recovers from the insanity of evil she may pray, but not now."

Chapter 15

Skeletons in William's Doctrinal Closet

I have often wondered what a writer of fiction would have made out of such a story as Mrs. Martin's. As a matter of fact, the woman is living today, highly respected, serenely proud of her two grown daughters; and I believe William simply covered up her sin so deep with his wisdom that she had forgotten it. His Methodist doctrinal closet has more than one skeleton like this in it.

"Repentance is not remorse," he used to argue upon rare occasions when I dragged them out. "Mrs. Martin could not make the proper distinction. God understood."

I have no doubt his conference would have fired him for fathering such curious heresies if all his dealings with sinners had been made public. There was the apostate, for example, whom he tried to save at the expense of one of the doctrines of his church.

Just as Baptists believe in election and Presbyterians in predestination, the Methodists believe in apostasy—that is, that

God will forsake a man and never answer his prayers if the man waits too long before he begins to pray; and that if after he has been converted he leaves the way of righteousness there is always danger that God will abandon him in his sins.

A most desperate situation is that of the Methodist apostate, because there is so much elasticity about grace in our church, and it is so easy to fall from grace that a modest man is, by the very humility of his spirit, likely to fall under the delusion that God has had enough patience with him, that he has "sinned away his day of grace."

I recall the day William came home and burned seven of his best sermons on such texts as this: "The soul that sinneth it shall die." It was after he had given the burial service over the body of Philip Hale, who killed himself because he had "lost God and could not find Him." Hale had been a Methodist, strictly brought up in that faith by parents who had had him baptized when he was an infant and who had kept the promise made then to bring him up in the "nurture and admonition of the Lord." They did, and he was converted at an early age before the tide of adolescence set in. It seems that he "sinned away his day of grace" during this dangerous period.

When William came on the circuit where he lived Hale was a sad, middle-aged man who spent much of his spare time looking for God and praying for the witness of the Spirit. Philip Hale was the most tragic figure I ever saw in the house of God. He was a large, dark man with a blasted look on his somber face. For years it was said that he was the first to accept the invitation for sinners to come to the altar for prayers and the last to leave it, always with that lost look—never blessed, never forgiven. William stood before him powerless. He could cast no light in that darkness; it was literally the outer darkness where light cannot be created. Toward the end of a revival, during which Hale had wandered back and forth from the altar night after night like a dazed sleepwalker, he went out and shot himself.

The fate of this man was one of the tragedies in William's life. He must have had much the same feeling toward him that a surgeon feels toward a patient who dies on the operating table. I never heard him preach after that about the "unpardonable sin" in the spiritual life.

One thing impressed me even more than it did William: he never was able to reach the chief sinners in his congregation. Some of them sat in high places in the church. Compared with these the reprobates on the back benches were easily stirred and awakened to a sense of their lost condition. Sometimes one of these members would confess to feeling "cold" spiritually, but I do not now recall a single one who really confessed his sins or renounced them.

Suppose a trustee owns a big flour mill and can afford to pay the preacher liberally, bear more than his share of the church budget and own an automobile besides, because he cheats every customer out of a few ounces of flour every time he weighs a purchase. What shall the pastor do—sacrifice the auto and the church needs? He never does, because at bottom he has a sneaking conviction that the car, in particular, is worth more than the trustee's kind of a soul, and he is shockingly correct in his estimate of values. If there really are any apostates in this world they belong to this spiritually- refrigerated class to be found in every religious denomination.

But if William did not close in often with the chief sinners, he occasionally came upon a rare saint. I mean "rare" in the scientific, spiritual sense—that is, different, moving in time, but not of it—the unconscious prophet of a new order in the souls of mankind. And it was a grand sight to see him measure the sword of his spirit with one of these.

The last encounter he had of this kind, I remember, was on the Bowtown Circuit not long before he was retired, and it was with a woman. She was called Sal Prout. The omission of the last syllable of her given name implied social ostracism and personal contempt. And she deserved both, having been notorious in her younger days.

We heard of her first from Brother Rheubottom. He was the shriveled, grizzled lay preacher who furnished a kind of gadfly gospel to the church at Bowtown when he was invited to fill the pulpit, which was no oftener than could be helped. He called to tell William about the "Prout woman" before we had had time to unpack our clothes and commentaries.

"She's been a terrible creature," he explained, wagging his hard old hickory- nut head and clawing his beard with a kind of spiritual rapacity for devouring the worst of Sal's character.

"She's done more harm than a dozen wildcat stills. Then all at once, here about five years ago she turned good, allowed she'd heerd from God. It was blasphemous. Seems she hadn't went to church since she was a gal. I don't say she ain't behavin' herself and all that, but 'tain't orthodox for a person like that to jest git religion without ever goin' nigh a church and makin' public confession of her sins—not that everybody don't know what she had been!

"If them kind of heresies spread, where will the church be? What's the use of havin' churches? We want you to go down there and 'tend to her, Brother Thompson. Some folks in this community have been worried ever since she done it.

"We ain't satisfied with her experience after the way she's carried on—talks as if she'd found God as easy as if she'd been an innocent child, when some of us that have lived honorable and decent all our lives had to mourn and repent and take on like a house afire before we could claim the blessin'."

"I'll look into Sister Prout's condition as soon as possible, Brother Rheubottom," said William, folding one long leg over the other and fidgeting in his chair, because he wanted to be back at his bookshelves, settling the relations of his commentaries for the coming year.

"She ain't even a sister," retorted our visitor, who had risen and was on his way to the door. "She's never j'ined the church. When somebody named it to her as a duty if she'd repented of her sins she jest laughed and said she wouldn't. Not bein' respectable enough to belong in with church folks she allowed she'd stay outside with the wicked where she belonged and not embarrass nobody by settin' by 'em in church. Allowed she reckoned she could find enough to do out there instead of hoisting herself up with respectable women in the foreign missionary society. That's the way she talks, Brother Thompson, and there can't nobody stop her!"

Bowtown was an ugly little streaked mountain village that followed the windings of the country road for half a mile and then gave out. The last house was not a house at all, but an old boxcar. And this was the home of Sal Prout. But she denied that it was a boxcar with a hundred fanciful deceptions. First, it was whitewashed within and without; second, it was covered with house vines; third, the dooryard smiled at you from the face of a thousand flowers, like a heavenly cataclysm of color. But go as often as we would we never found Sal at home. She was busy with the wicked. She could do anything from pulling fodder to nursing a teething baby, and all you had to do to get her was to need her.

This was how we came to meet her at last. William's health was failing fast now, and he got down with rheumatism that spring. He had been in bed a month; the people on the circuit began to show they were disappointed in not having an active man who could fill his appointments, and I was tired and discouraged with being up so much at night and with anxiety for fear William would have to give up his work.

A preacher in our church cannot get even the little it affords from the retirement fund until he has been on the retired list a year; and if he gives up his work in the middle of the previous year that means he must go eighteen months without resources. That is a long time when you have not been able to save anything and when you are old and sick.

So, I was sitting in the kitchen door of the parsonage one morning after William had had a particularly bad night, wondering what God was going to do about it, for I knew we could not expect help from any other source. The agnostics may say what they please, but if you get cornered between old age and starvation you will find out that there is a real sure-enough good God who numbers the remaining hairs of your head and counts the sparrows' fall. William and I tried Him, and we know. There were terrible times toward the last when we never could have made it if it had not been for God.

And I reckon that morning was one of the "terrible times," for as I was sitting there wondering sadly what would happen next, an immense woman came around the corner of the house and stood before me on the doorstep. She was past fifty years of age, and had the appearance of a dismantled woman. Nothing of youth or loveliness remained. I have never seen a face so wrecked with wrinkles, so marred with frightful histories—yet there was a kind of fairness over all her ruins.

"I am Sal Prout," she said, and it was so deep and rich a voice that it was as if one of the bare brown hills of the earth had spoken to me. "And I've come to git breakfast," she added, spreading peace over her dreadful face with an ineffable smile.

An hour later she was in possession of William and me and the parsonage. She was clearing up the breakfast things when she said, "You look tired; go an git some rest. I'll take care of him," nodding her head toward the door of William's room.

When I awakened in the middle of the afternoon he was sitting up against four hot-water bottles, letting her call him "Brother Billy." That sounds scandalous, but listening from where I lay on the sofa in the front room I could tell that they were having a duel of spirits, and that she was taking liberties with William's theology that must have made his guardian angel pale.

He wore his red flannel nightshirt, had a quilt folded around his legs and one of Benson's commentaries open upon his knees. His hair was brushed in fine style, and his long beard lay like a stole upon his breast. His hands were resting on the arms of his chair, and he was regarding Sal, who sat in the opposite corner openly dipping snuff, with a kind of fascinated disapproval.

"The kind of faith you have in God don't do Him jestice," she was saying. "It's sorter infernal—it's so mean and partial. Your God ain't nothing but a paradise capitalist and aristocrat—the sort of one that fixes up a flower garden for Him and jest His saints to set in the middle of and sing and harp on their harps, while a right smart chance of the best folks sneak and shuffle around in the outer darkness forever because, like me, they had no chance to be good, and so went wrong before they knowed where they were going. Sometimes these last years since I had my vision of God, I've wanted to tell you preachers that the little ornamental divinity that you shout about ain't nothing but a figger of speech took from the heathens and made over by heathen Christians."

"Stop!" said William, lifting one of his thin, white hands and waving it imperatively at her. "You must not speak irreverently. I know you don't mean it, but ..."

"Jest answer me this, sir—is your leg hurtin' any worse?"

"No," replied William, mollified.

"Not a mite?" she insisted.

"No, I am much easier of the pain."

"Well, then, I'm goin' to say this much more even if it strangles you. The word "God" stands for something in the hearts of men and women bigger'n a paradise gardener with a taste for music!"

"You don't put it fair, Sister Prout," said William, aggrieved.

"I can't put it in as fine language as Saint John, if that's what you mean."

"What is the nature of God as you see Him?" asked William.

We are made very different in the soul, not nearly so much alike as we are in other respects. I saw now the same light pass over Sal's face that I had often seen in William's, yet they could not agree about their own heavenly Father.

"The God I trust is the One that makes flowers like them bloom for sech as me," she began, pointing through the window at a rose; "that lets His rain fall in my garden same as He does in your'n; that never takes His spite out on me for bein' what I was, but jest made it hard for me and waited patient for me. He's the kind of God, sir, that can change a heart like mine from all the evil there is and make it so I can think good thoughts and be kind, and enjoy His hills and hear the birds sing again, same as

I used to pay attention to 'em when I was a little gal."

She lowered her voice as if speaking of a mortal sorrow. "There were years and years, sir, when them little creatures were singin' all around me every day, but I couldn't hear 'em—my deeds were so evil. I don't reckon you know it—livin' the little you have—but sin affects you that way—takes away your hearin' for sweet sounds, your sight for what is lovely. But God, He jest kept on lettin' His birds sing for me, and the sun riz jest as fine above the hills behind my house. He didn't pick at me, nor put a sign on me same as folks did of my shame, as He could have done with a cloud or something over my house. You see, He'd fixed things from the foundations of the world so as they'd work out good and not evil for us every one, beca'se He knowed we'd all git tired and come home some time, the same as I've come. I don't know whether you ever found it out or not, sir, but sinners git awful tired of sinnin'. God knows that. He knows they just can't keep it up forever!"

The next winter Sal Prout died of smallpox, after nursing a community of sawmill hands farther up in the mountains who had been stricken with the disease, and many of whom might have died but for her care.

William never recovered from that attack of rheumatism. His legs got well, but he did not. He was different afterward, as if he had fallen into a trance. He seemed always to look and speak across a space of which he was not conscious. He filled his appointments after a fashion during the remainder of the year at the Bowtown district, but he grew increasingly forgetful of people and all earthly considerations. Sometimes he fell to dreaming in the middle of his sermon, looking over the heads of his congregation as if he were expecting Noah's dove to bring him a token or Michael the archangel to blow his trumpet. Then again he would make his prayer longer than his sermon. The people did not like it, and the presiding elder called for his retirement at the conference that fall, on the grounds that Brother Thompson showed signs of "failing powers."

Maybe he did, but it was only his mortal faculties that were failing. To the last he retained a clear and definite knowledge of the kingdom of heaven that many a man in possession of all his powers never attains. The great change was that he took on a melancholy attitude to reality.

Chapter 16

In the Little Graveyard Behind Redwine Church

William was too dazed by the misfortune of his forced retirement to think or plan for the future. For him there was no future. He sat in the chimney corner, following me about the house with his vacant eyes. He was grieving for one of the choice, hard circuits, with its dried-fruit salary, such as he had received for years, or remembering the good pastoral times he had had in one of this or that year past.

I have sometimes wondered what would be the moral effect upon a church community if an old and helpless preacher like William should be sent to it with the understanding that the church should minister to him instead of his ministering to the church; that every saint and sinner should be invited to contribute to his peace and comfort, even as for years he had labored for them. There would be less preaching, of course, but more development in real Christian service. An old preacher treated in this manner would become very dictatorial, a perfect autocrat about ordering charities for the poor and prayers for the penitents, but would it be so bad for the church?

However, that was not my consideration now. The Redwine Circuit where we had begun our life together was only twenty miles distant; the little house between the two green hills that had been the Methodist parsonage thirty years before was long since abandoned for a shiny, green and yellow spindle-legged new parsonage at Royden. And while William, who had always had his home dictated to him by the conference, showed a pathetic apathy about choosing one for himself, I hankered for the ragged-roofed cottage with its ugly old chimneys that had first sheltered our life together. So within a month the horse and buggy were sold, the cottage at Redwine rented, and we settled in it like two crippled birds in a half-feathered nest.

Now, for the first time since I left Edenton, a happy, thoughtless bride, I had leisure to think just of ourselves, of our sum total as it were. And I found that we were two human numerals added together for a lifetime which made a deficit.

Yet we had not been idle or indifferent workers. For thirty years William had been in the itinerancy, filling nearly every third and fourth class appointment in his conference. He had preached over three thousand sermons, baptized more than four hundred infants, received nearly four thousand souls into membership. He had been untiring in his efforts to raise his apportionments and had paid more pastoral calls than half a dozen doctors need to make in order to become famous and wealthy.

Time changed us; we grew old. I abandoned my waistline to nature's will and my face settled into the expression of a good negative that has been blurred by too long exposure to a strong light. Toward the end William looked like the skin-and-bones remnant of a saint. His face was sunken and hollowed out till the very Wesley in him showed through. His beard was long and had whitened until it gave his Moses-head the appearance of coming up out of a holy mist.

So, I say, we aged; but we went on from circuit to circuit with no other change except that when we saved enough money William bought a new horse. It was a terrible treadmill, and we could expect no reward or change in this world, no promotion, no ease of mind except the ease of prayers, which I never enjoyed as much as William did. I had feelings that prayers did not put down the desires they did not satisfy. There were times when I almost hated prayers, when I had a mortal aversion to heaven and wished only that God would give me a long earth-rest of the spirit.

We found the same kind of sinners everywhere and the same defects in all the saints. Sometimes I even wished someone would develop a new sort of wickedness, a kind that would vary the dreadful monotony of repentance and cause William to scratch his theological head for a different kind of sermon. But no one ever did. Whether we were in the mountains or in the towns, among the rich or the poor, the people transgressed by the same mortal actions and fell short of the glory of God exactly alike.

At last I came to understand that there is just one kind of sin in the world—the sin against love—and no saints at all. I can't say that I was disappointed, but I was just tired of the awful upward strain of trying to develop faculties and feelings suitable to another world yet have to be living in this one.

And to make things worse, William took on a weary look after his retirement, like that of a man who has made a long journey in vain. This is always the last definition the itinerancy writes upon the faces of its retired preachers. They are unhappy, mortified, like honorable men who have failed in a business. They no longer pretend to have better health than they really have, which is the pathetic hypocrisy they all practice toward the last when they are in annual fear of retirement.

So, I looked at our deficit and knew that something was wrong. Still, I went about the little old house and garden, trying to reconstruct the memory of happiness and planning to spend our last days unharassed by salvation anxieties. I have never doubted the goodness of God, but things being as they are, and we being what we are, it takes a long time for Him to work it out for us, especially in any kind of a church.

Meanwhile, I tried to find some of our old friends, only to discover that most of them were dead. I planted a few annuals, set some hens and prepared to cultivate my own peace. But William was changed. He had lost his courage. Whenever rheumatism struck him he gave in to it with a groan. Then he took up with Job in the Scriptures, and before we had been back long enough for the flowers to bloom he just turned over his spiritual ash heap and died.

He is buried in the little graveyard behind Redwine Church, along with most of the men and women to whom he had preached thirty years ago.

I can feel that I am not setting things down right, not making the latitude and longitude of experience clearly so that you may see as I can when I close my eyes the staggering tombstones in the brown shadows behind the little brown church. But when one has been in the Methodist itinerancy a lifetime one cannot do that.

I used to wonder why Paul, passing through all the grandest cities and civilizations of his time, never left behind him a single description of any of their glories, only a reference to the altar "To The Unknown God" that he found in Athens; but now I know. Paul lost the memory of sight. He had absent-minded eyes to the things of the world. So it is with the itinerant. The earth becomes one of the stars. I cannot remember roads and realities. I recall most clearly only spiritual facts, like this: Timothy Brown was a bad man, soundly converted under William's ministry, but how he looked, on which circuit he lived, I have long ago forgotten.

In spite of my well-settled, worldly mind, William prayed away its foundations during those thirty years together, until now the very scene of his passing floats as a mist in my memory. I know he lay in the same house where he had brought me on our wedding day. Through the window in the pearl light of the early morning there was the same freshness upon the hills, the same streams glistening like silver between. There was the same little valley below, closed in like a cup, filled with corn and honey and bees and flowers. The same gray farmhouses brooded close to the earth, with children playing in the dooryards. It was all there the morning he died, as it had been that blue and glad morning thirty years before; but I could not see it or feel it, with him lying stretched and still upon the bed with the sheet drawn over his face, and the people crowding in, whispering, shuffling, bearing the long, black coffin with them. It is dim and blurred and I cannot think it or write it properly. There seemed a hoarfrost upon the window-panes; the hills were bare, and the cup of the valley lay drained and empty before me, with the shadow of death darkening all the light of day.

A very old woman, bent, shriveled down to her skin and bones, with her thin lips sucked in between her gums, came and tugged at my sleeve. I recognized Sister Glory White, bearing the same air of rapacious cheerfulness that she used to wear upon her fat face when she had a "body" to prepare for burial.

"Come, Sister Thompson, you must git up and go out. We air ready to lay him out now."

"Oh, not him!" I cried. "You have laid out so many. Let someone else do it!" For I could not forget the frightful pleasure she had taken years ago in her ghoulish task.

"And why not him? I've helped to put away every man, woman and child that has died in this settlement since I was grown, and I ain't goin' to shirk my duty to Brother Thompson—not that I ever expected to do it for him." She babbled on, gently urging me from the room, where her presence was the last blinding touch of horror for me.

*   *   *   *   *   *   *   *   *   *   *

So far, my autobiography has been mixed with William's biography, just as my life seems to mingle with the dust in his grave. But I came to an experience now of my own, unglorified by William, so strange that I cannot explain it unless there is what may be called a reversion of type in spirit, like this: that a person may be absolutely dominated for years by certain influences and not only feel no antagonism to them, but actually yield with devotion and inconceivable sacrifices. Yet, when the influence is removed and there is no longer the love-cause for faithfulness the illusion not only passes, but the person finds himself of his original mind and spirit, emancipated, gone back to himself—what he really was in the beginning before the domination began. Such at least is as nearly what now happened to me as I can tell it.

I remained in the little house between the hills, walking about, attending to my few wants, receiving an occasional visitor in a sort of trance of sorrow. William had always meant more to me than heaven. I had endured poverty, prayers, persecutions and revivals for his sake. And now I had lost him. The very thought was unbearable. I wore it for mourning. I missed him when I looked down the bridle path into the valley, and I missed him when I looked at the stars. Nothing meant anything to me without him.

Then suddenly the veil lifted. I seemed at last to have surrendered him to what is beyond the grave. At once my own mind came back to me; not the humble, church-censored mind I had during his life, but my very own, and it was like another conversion. I remembered scenes and thoughts and faces that I had not recalled since girlhood. The innocent gaiety of my youth came back to me, and I recalled distinctly with what naive, happy worldliness I faced the world then, and not the kingdom of heaven that I had been staring through William's eyes for the thirty years since.

The next Sunday I went to church as usual, but I did not go up near the front, which had always been my custom. It occurred to me that now I did not have to sit in the saints' neighborhood, but might sit back with the more honest human beings. The preacher was a young man of the progressive new order, who sustained the same relation as pastor to the church that an ambitious foreman sustains to a business that must be renovated and improved. He was taking up his foreign missionary collection very much after the manner of an auctioneer.

"Five dollars, five dollars, five dollars: who gives five dollars that the gospel may be spread in China and Siam? Who gives five dollars that there may be light in India and to save women from casting their innocent babes into the Ganges? Thank you, Sister Tuttle. The women are leading off, getting ahead of you, brethren. Put down five dollars from Sister Tuttle. Now, who will give four dollars?" and so on down till even the sinners on the back benches subscribed a rattle of dimes.

I listened with comfortable indifference. I thought of how William died without enough oil in him to grease his joints. And how many more like him had died too weak and depleted to have even assurance of their own salvation. I remembered how I wished toward the last that I could afford a few delicacies, for William liked a bit of liqueur and real cream, which might have strengthened and cheered him.

Then and there I resolved never to give another cent to foreign missions. I am not opposed to foreign missions, you understand. William and I did without much that the heathen might have missionaries who would bring the gospel to them. But that is just it. We did without too much. I am not saying that anyone else ought to lessen their contribution to missions. Let others give even more. But I am certain they ought to treble their contribution to old preachers.

There is something fearful in the Bible like this, "But if any provide not for his own, and especially for those of his own house, he hath denied the faith and is worse than an infidel." That Scripture expressed my feelings exactly as I listened to the preacher take up his foreign missionary collection and remembered William's dreadful poverty. So, I say, I made up my own private mind that there is something wrong with the way church collections are distributed, and that if I ever had any spare money it should be devoted to purchasing a taller tombstone for William.

Immediately I felt my own "I am," sitting up in me and taking courage. It was a soaring sensation. For so many years I had not belonged to myself. I was simply a prayer-meeting numeral, William's personal dynamo at the women's societies. Suddenly it came to me that I was a free moral agent for the first time in my life—widows are the only women who are.

This scandalous reflection took hold of me as I listened to the collection and reflected that never again would I have to worry lest William fail to raise all his apportionments, that I should never be anxious now for fear his sermons might not please the prominent members of his church. But the most refreshing, rejuvenating of all was the thought that at last I could be a little less good. I looked at the awkward men and women sitting in still rows across the little church, with their faces lit like candles from the preacher's face, and I experienced a peaceful remoteness from them and from the pulpit light.

Chapter 17

Back Again to the World

Sometimes I wonder if the carnal man ever dies in us, or the carnal woman either, for that matter. We only say so in our prayers and rituals because we do not know yet how to be spiritually truthful about our own mortal frailties. But God, who knew very well what He was about when He made us human, sees to it that in spite of our flagrant pretensions we remain honest Adams and Eves to the end. So, for years, without acknowledging it to myself, I had been homesick for the world and the things of the world. I did not want to "sin," I simply longed to be natural; to live a trifle less rigidly in my soul.

There had been so many prayer-meeting nights when I would rather have been at the grand opera. Not that William's prayer-meeting talks were not the very bread of life—they were; but there is such a thing as losing one's appetite for just one kind of bread. I have always thought one of the notable things about the Israelites' journey through the wilderness was the amazing fortitude with which they accepted their manna diet. Anyhow, it is not in the power of words to tell how I pined for the real laughter and lightness and play of life.

William had needed them no less, but the difference was he never knew it. When he felt world-hungry he thought it was a sign of spiritual anemia and prayed for a closer walk with God—as if God were not also the God of the world even more than He is the deity of any church or creed. I am not reflecting on William in saying this—I'd sooner reflect upon one of the crown jewels of heaven, but I am reflecting upon his understanding. It was not sufficiently earthly—no good priest's is. Still, I had been his faithful wife for thirty years and a consistent member of a church which forbids nearly every form of amusement other than a Sunday school picnic, a church festival or a Methodist youth meeting.

I did not wait to speak to the people after the sermon, the way a preacher's wife must do to show her friendliness and interest. I hurried out and around behind the church to where William lay folded deep beneath the pine shadows. And there I had it out with him, as sometimes we had it out together in other days, I doing all the talking, and he no less silent than usual there in his holy grave. We had never quarreled as man and wife because he would not do his part of the contending. I untied my bonnet, took it off and laid it on the grass, sat down by his headstone and cried—not so much for him as for fear he would not understand. He never had.

William's greatest limitation as a minister was his firm conviction that the world was a hindrance on our journey to heaven. He fought and abused the world to the last, as if God had not made it and designed it to furnish properly- chastened material for His higher kingdom. And somehow, as I wept and talked down to William in his dust, I felt wonderfully like the young woman who had loved him and feared him during those first rebellious years when I was still so much the Episcopalian and so little the Methodist.

The next day I sent a letter to my sister Sarah, a widow living with her two grown daughters in New York. For years I had kept up no relations with my own family. They were of the world—prosperous—and I felt that they could not understand

William nor the uncompromising way we lived. But now I was writing to accept the invitation Sarah sent me just after William's death to make my home with her.

A week later I packed my things, took my church membership letter, locked my door and took the train at Royden for New York. I told the neighbors I was going for a visit to New York, but really I was on my way to find the world again. And I found it. You cannot find anything else in New York.

Sarah and the girls met me at the Grand Central Station and they spent more kisses welcoming me than I had received since my bridal days.

Sarah is two years older than I am, but she looks ten years younger, and there is not the mark of a prayer on her smooth face, while I feel as if I might have the doxology stamped in wrinkles above my eyebrows.

Now everything is different from the way it was at home. We do not have dinner till suppertime, and there is no mantel or fireplace in my room, although the furniture is grander than anything I ever saw. I set William's photograph on the dresser, and I can tell by the way he looks at me all day long that he would not approve of the way I am carrying on. But I cannot help it; I must have a little fling of world-life. That other in which I qualified with him for heaven was too stretching and something in me grew mortally tired of stretching. I have set myself with all diligence to enjoy the things of this world in the time that's left me. The more I think of it the more nearly certain I am that these pleasures were meant for us.

One thing alone troubles me—that is, the thought of William going up and down these thirty years just preaching and praying and bearing other people's burdens and never once having the right to step aside and rest his soul from being just good; never once having an ordinary human vacation in the natural, human world; always praying and preaching and fasting that he might pray and preach better, always scrimping that he might be able to pay more to the cause of missions, always a little threadbare, and often a little breathless spiritually, but always persistently stalking Peter and Paul and the angels through the Scriptures, up the high and higher altitudes of his own beautiful imagination. No matter how rested he is now in heaven, no matter how much he may be enjoying himself, my heart aches for him because of the innocent happiness he missed here.

Sometimes when I am with Sarah's girls at a play like Sudermann's "John the Baptist," and the curtain rises and falls upon the great scenes, I sit and think of William and what it would have meant to him if in all those poverty- stricken years of his ministry he could have had such a vision of his dear Bible people at home in the Promised Land. It's foolish, of course, but I still long to do something for him, something to make up for the weariness and blindness through which he passed with such simple dignity up to God, who never meant for him to make such a hard journey of it. No one knew it, probably, save a few of the angels, but he was a great man.

Since I have been here where everybody and every thought of everybody is so different from William and his thinking, I can see him more clearly and understand him better than I did living side by side with him. This is why I have been spending my time between tea parties and lectures on art and evolution, and receptions and theaters, writing these letters as a memorial of him.

I used to wish I could have a great artist paint a portrait of William as he looked sometimes on a Sabbath day when he had a baby to baptize, or when he'd be bending over an altar full of penitents. There was a grandeur in William's faith that gave him, at such times, an awesome likeness to immortality even in his flesh. But, of course, I could never afford the portrait, so in these letters I have tried to draw a likeness of him. Every line and shadow of it is as true as I can make it to what he really was. I know many people back there on his circuits will recognize it, although I have changed names so as not to be too personal. They will remember him, although he was not what is known as an up-to-date preacher.

Since I have been in New York I have thought of many things

that William didn't know or even dream of. I never heard him mention evolution. His doubts were not intellectual and his troubles were solely spiritual. He never suspected that there were two Isaiahs, never discovered that David did not write his own Psalms, or that Genesis was considered a fable, never noticed anything queer about the way Moses kept on writing about himself after he was dead and his death certificate properly recorded by himself in the Scriptures. William was a man of faith. All of his ideas came out of that one little mustard seed. I doubt if he'd have been surprised if some day he had come upon a burning bush along one of the bridle paths of his circuit.

As for me, I do not care what they say here in New York, or even in the Pentateuch, I'd have a sight more confidence in that reference of the burning bush if William had recorded it instead of Moses—I never set much store by Moses as a truth teller. He may have been a good hand at chiseling out the Ten Commandments in the tables of stone, and he may have been strong enough to tote them down by himself from Sinai, but Moses was too much of a hero to tell the truth and nothing but the truth about himself. I never knew a hero who could do it. Their courage gets mixed with their imagination.

You realize that I could not write about a man like William in the modern, forked-lightning literary style, as if he were a new brand of spiritual soap or the dime-novel hero of a fashionable congregation. The people he served were not like those in New York, who appear to have been created by electricity, with a spiritual button for a soul that you press into a religious fervor by rendering an organ opera behind the pulpit. Or maybe the preacher does it with a new-fangled notion that demonstrates a scientific relation between some other life and this one.

The people William served were backwoods and mountain folk, for the most part, who grew out of the soil and were as much a part of it as the red oaks and the hills. They were not happy nor good, but they were scriptural. The men were in solemn bondage to heaven. Religion was a sort of life sentence they worked out with painful diligence. And the women seemed "born again" just to fade and pray, not as these women of the world fade, utterly, but fade like fair tea- roses plucked for an altar that soon wither. In heaven you will not find them herded in the Hosannah Chorus with the great, good women of history like Jane Addams and Frances E. Willard, but they will be there in some dim cove of the celestial hills spinning love upon the distaffs of heaven, weaving yarn feathers for the younger angels.

I say, it is impossible to write of such a preacher and such people as if they were characters in a religious fantasy. Walking to and from church here in this city I have almost wondered if they were ever real. Thinking of them sets me to recalling stanzas from Isaac Watts' hymns.

I smell the thyme upon their hills. It seems as if my adjectives were beginning to grow like flowers upon William's grave. I can see the candles lit for evening services in heaven, and him sitting in the Amen Corner away from the flashing-winged, fashionable saints, comparing notes with Moses and Elijah in his deep, organ voice.

The trouble with William was that he was the hero of another world yet living in this one, handcuffed by a church discipline. And the trouble with the average New York preacher is that he is barely a foreigner in this world, who is apologizing continually to his congregation for half-way believing what he is preaching.

But now I have finished this imperfect drawing of William's character. If I could have made it enough like him it might have been fit for one of the family portraits of the saints in heaven. I have often wondered why the monument builders have never thought to raise a statue to the Methodist circuit rider. The Daughters of the American Revolution and the other daughters of this and that raise monuments to men who were only brave, but no one has thought yet to erect a statue to the memory of the Methodist circuit riders, who are no less brave, but who have doubtless broken some heavenly records in simple goodness and self-sacrifice.

Chapter 18

Conscientious Scruples About the Church

I had thought these letters were finished, but I am adding this postscript to say that I leave New York tomorrow for the little house between the hills on the Redwine Circuit. This resolution is not in keeping with some views and sentiments I have written in these pages, but being a woman, I thank God I can be as inconsistent as is necessary to feminine peace of mind. I imagine I'll never be satisfied now, neither in the world nor in the church without William. I can't seem to settle into any state of being of my own. I am not saying that I have not had a good time here, but after all, I do not belong with the people of the world either.

Since I have been with Sarah I have had constantly to resist the temptation to speak to her about her soul, just from force of habit. I have never seen, in all my years with William, a woman of her age so youthfully, cheerfully unconscious of having a soul. And that is not the worst of it. I can feel my moral elbows sticking out in every conversation, as if heaven had made all my thoughts angular. It is a sort of rugged integrity that grows up in a woman who follows the gospel flag of the Methodist itinerancy.

I am sure it is often embarrassing to Sarah and the girls, especially when they have company, not the kind of company William and I had—thinly-bred missionaries and Bible peddlers, tramps and beggars, and occasionally, toward the last a little, sweet-faced, empty-headed deaconess—but society ladies and one or two that William would call "Delilahs," and handsome, sleek, intellectual men who appeared to be as ignorant of God as I am of natural history. I am not saying that they are not decent people, but they are not all there. I miss something out of them. If they have ever had souls they have had them removed, probably by a kind of reasoning surgery quite as effective as the literal surgery with which so many of them have their inflamed appendixes removed.

I have told Sarah I am leaving, and while she expresses regret I am sure she feels relieved. It is a strain to have a person in the family who belongs to a different spiritual species. And now I have just finished packing my things. I am thankful I told the neighbors that I was going for a visit. I came suddenly to the conclusion today that it was only a visit because of a thing that happened. I have not been offended morally by anything I have seen in the theaters or other places of amusement, but I have had conscientious scruples about the churches here!

This would be the Sabbath day far away in the country, where the hills are at prayer and the pine trees swing their shadows over the graves in Redwine churchyard. But here in New York it is merely the day when you change your occupations and amusements. Still, there is preaching for those who are not drunk or asleep or in the parks or at Coney Island or giving weekend parties at their country places or planning the millennium without God along superficial socialistic reasoning and barbed-wire theories of the brotherhood of man.

I always went with the girls to their fashionable church. And this is how the morals in me that William planted came to take offense, and how I reached the conclusion that I had best go back home where life is indeed made too hard for the spirit, but where at least one may be decently conscious of having a soul according to the Scriptures.

The church we attended was nearly as grand looking inside as a theater. Every pew was filled, and there was no misbehavior on the back benches such as William contended with to the last. We had a covered pew near the front, and a stool to put our feet on, and a library hooked to the back of the pew in front of us containing a bulletin of the church news. I didn't have time to find the "society column," but I was looking for it when the preacher came in.

I expected to hear a perfectly-scarifying sermon, he looked so much like a tintype of the prophet Jeremiah; but he took his text from Mark about the healing of the man with the withered hand, and preached on the hypnotism of Jesus. He made a clean sweep of the miracles in the most elegant, convincing language you ever heard. And I sat and cried to think of what he'd done to Scriptures William would have cried to preserve. The girls were mortified at the scene I was making. I don't reckon anybody had ever cried in that church before, and I am sure no man was ever convicted of his sins there.

When we reached home I told Sarah about going back to Redwine first thing. Then I came on upstairs and had it out with William in a very few words, while I was pulling out the dresser drawers and putting my things in the trunk.

"William," I said, kneeling down on the floor with my back to his picture on my dresser (while packing my collars), "you were right. There is something wrong with the institutional religion that the church is propagating; but there is nothing wrong with the truth of God for which you stood and made me stand for thirty years, and I am going back where some of the people know it, whether they know anything else or not.

"Up here the best, the wisest people don't know what the truth of God is—they think they can find it in science. Faith is for fools who cannot think. They are not trying to reconcile God to man, but man to God, and are trimming down the Holy Ghost to suit their superficial scientific faculties."

Then I reached back, snatched up William's photo, laid it bottom-up on top of the collars. I didn't feel that I could look him squarely in the face till I had it setting back on the mantel in the house at Redwine.

I have got the first out-and-out orthodox Methodist feeling of being backslidden I ever had in my life. And it was not going to the theaters and tea parties that brought it on. It was going to church every Sunday and hearing some preacher explain away the divinity of Jesus or reduce His miracles to scientific formulas.

I do not wonder that so many men and women go wrong in New York. They are orphans, deprived of their heavenly Father by the very preachers themselves. And it's very hard for orphans to behave themselves. They know what is right, but righteousness does not appeal to them because it has never been sanctified by love.

That is what is the matter with these people. They do not love God, they do not care, or know, or believe that He loves them. They are so sensible, so profoundly reasonable that they are sadly damned already by their own little intelligences. They have theories, views and knowledges that are not going to show up well in the next generation. And that is their crime, to propagate ideas that will destroy the integrity of those who will come after them.